Pen-Ultimate II:

A Speculative Fiction Anthology

Edited by
Talib S. Hussain and LJ Cohen

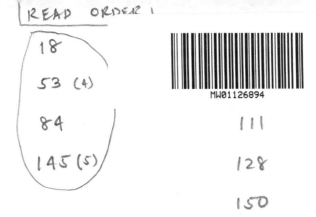

!?*Interrobang Books*

Pen-Ultimate II: A Speculative Fiction Anthology

edited by Talib S. Hussain and LJ Cohen

Published by Interrobang Books
Newton, MA

First print edition: July 2016

ISBN-13: 978-1-942851-02-8
ISBN-10: 1-942851-02-2

Original cover art © 2016 by Chris Howard
www.saltwaterwitch.com

Once more, for our mentors:
Jeffrey A. Carver and Craig Shaw Gardner

Contents

Part II: Confusion and Change

Foreword

Three years ago, we pulled together our first *Pen-Ultimate* anthology of speculative fiction. Our goal was to provide an opportunity for authors in our extended writing community—graduates of the Boston area Ultimate Science Fiction Writing Workshop—to share their stories. With the encouragement of our mentors, Jeffrey Carver and Craig Shaw Gardner, who had taught all of us, we collaboratively and iteratively workshopped our stories till they shined, and finally put our completed anthology out in the wide world for public consumption. The two of us so thoroughly loved the process and the outcome that we decided to do it again. So, here for your reading pleasure is our *Pen-Ultimate II* anthology with 16 stories by 12 authors from our community.

Herein, you'll find stories that explore possible futures where lifespans are diminishing (*Spira Mirabilis*), where civilization is all but gone (*North*), where humanity is influenced by an alien life-form (*Botanical Difficulties*) or where we face the eventual end of our solar system (*Burning Time*). In worlds not too dissimilar to our own, you'll read about movers and shakers who take debts seriously (*A Night at The Broken Hourglass*), lurking monsters (*The Lurker*), a man who can live in the subsecond (*Frozen Moments*), and visitors we lost the opportunity to meet (*Sputnik 2, Interior*). You'll experience dreams of love that are virtual (*Our Abstract World*), doubt-filled (*Graveyard Shift*) and continually shifting (*Sweet Dreams*). And, you'll reflect on the consequences of choices, from divine interventions (*For the Sake*; *A Photograph of Silver Moonlight on Black Water*) and not-so-divine retribution (*The Playground*) to the harsh realities of survival (*Road to Redemption*) and repercussions of thoughtless actions (*The Harvest*).

So, welcome to new readers, and hello once again to returning ones. We hope you gain hours of enjoyment from these tales, and that you feel inspired in turn to pursue your own intellectual and artistic pursuits—whether for yourself or for and with friends and colleagues. It's worth it!

Talib S. Hussain and LJ Cohen
July 24, 2016

Part I:
Challenge and Choice

Sputnik 2, Interior

KJ Kabza

We were almost not alone.

On a frigid day in 1957, Sputnik 2 went up on a Sputnik-PS rocket. You remember Sputnik 2. SOVIET FIRES NEW SATELLITE, CARRYING DOG, the newspapers said, back when there were newspapers.

We read about it in sixth grade. Our textbooks said Laika the dog orbited the earth for days and passed away gently, peacefully; man's best friend a benevolent sacrifice to the stars.

But now we know our childhood textbooks lied. FIRST DOG IN SPACE DIED WITHIN HOURS, the Internet said, almost fifty years later. A man in Moscow had dug up and analyzed Laika's telemetry data. No life signs had been detected from the capsule after the first five to seven hours, he said. She perished from panic and overheating. He showed us the tracings of her racing heart and the soaring temperatures in the cabin.

What race of monsters dooms best friends to this?

The Others considered this question, watching us watch Laika die.

Her corpse orbited our pale blue dot for less than a year before Sputnik 2 fell.

The Others fly further and further away.

KJ Kabza *began selling short fiction in 2002, while earning his B.A. in Creative Writing from Antioch College. Since then, he has sold over 60 stories to places such as* Fantasy & Science Fiction, Beneath Ceaseless Skies, Daily Science Fiction, The Year's Best Dark Fantasy and Horror 2014, The Best Horror of the Year, Volume Six, *and more. His work has been called, "Intelligent and sublime—a powerful combination" (*Tangent*), "Fascinating, unique, imaginative" (*SFRevu*), and "Worthy of Edgar Allan Poe" (*SFcrowsnest*). Sign up for his mailing list or follow him on Twitter to receive news and alerts on newly-released fiction.*

Mailing list: http://eepurl.com/27xTr
Twitter: https://twitter.com/kjkabza
Homepage: http://kjkabza.com/index.html
Amazon Author Page:
http://www.amazon.com/author/kjkabza
Smashwords Author Page:
https://www.smashwords.com/profile/view/KJKabza

A Night at The Broken Hourglass

Chad Kroll

I gave the knock and the eye slit slid open. A bass so low you could hear it in your chest grunted, "Password?"

"Grant's Tomb," I replied. The slit closed and, after what sounded like an I-beam being dragged back, the grimy door opened about three feet. I barely edged through before it slammed shut again.

Standing in the antechamber, I was acutely aware of the size of Turk the doorman. A massive form in a tux. Even in the dim light I saw his thick brow and catcher's mitt hands. He was a study in brute force, as those who tried to enter without waiting could attest. The story was his grandmother had taken refuge from a storm under the wrong bridge in the old country. Grandpappy was no mortal toll collector; that was for sure. Not that anyone would ask. The Mason jar of teeth on a shelf next to his reinforced stool would shut the yap of even the most gin-soaked patron.

Turk moved past me, filling the small space. He pulled back the heavy velvet curtain that kept the foyer from where the real action was.

"Enjoy ya evenin'," he said.

"Thanks," I replied with a nod of my head and stepped into the lounge. I felt the curtain fall back behind me. The glamour dropped and the light and noise increased immediately. Here was the high-pitched laughter of a peroxide doxy, the rhythmic hiss of crushed ice in a shaker, and Fintan "Lamentation" Hayes on the piano. A young Irishman, he had a sound rife with peat and sorrow one moment and full of bluster and Gaelic charm the next.

I grabbed a small two-top and waited for the attention of Maxine, the cocktail waitress who was on tonight. The only thing faster than her delivery was her chatter. It was a good thing she didn't charge by the word, or I couldn't afford to drink here.

"Well, Mister St. Clair, good to see you again, how've you been, good I hope, what can I get cha'?" Her words fired away before her shadow came across the table.

"Good, Maxine. You?"

Three words in and a full response, not too shabby.

"Great, thanks for asking, Mister St. Clair. Busy, busy, busy. Always a drink or a light needed. Good thing, too. Keeps me off the bread lines, know what I mean, Mister St. Clair?"

"I do, Maxine. Whatever Beau's—"

"Gotcha, Mister St. Clair, be right back." And off she went, having three conversations on the way to the bar. A human hummingbird. If she ever got canned, she could auctioneer or call the races.

The bar itself was an imposing piece of art—a carefully carved dark wooden altar. The gentleman behind it was a Confederate confessor to the worldly worshippers. Blond, lantern-jawed, and possessing a posture that school marms would approve of, Beauregard "Beau" Remington was every bit the young southern gentleman. Only his fashion sense, including his non-oiled hair with his trademark sideburns, gave away his antebellum age.

Well, any spirit that served spirits as well as he did was entitled to his own peculiarities. Just don't bring up "The War of Northern Aggression," a sore spot that'd only lead to getting a watered-down drink or a "Mickey" that'd make you wish you were as dead as Beau was, depending on how much you offended his honor.

Maxine gave him the order and flicked a thumb back towards my table. Beau leaned around a rummy that was telling an animated tale and gave me a quick wink. He reached for one bottle off the top shelf, and one from under the bar itself. One of his "over-unders" then: the smoothness of refined liquor with the kick of rotgut hooch. He grabbed a small canister from one of the alcoves carved into the bar and added a dash of powder to the mix. He then poured it neatly into a highball glass and sent it via Maxine to me.

"Try this on for size," she quipped as she sped by.

The amber cocktail was unusually warm to the touch. I looked into the glass by the light of the small candle on the table. The drink swirled with smoke and sparks that flickered in the liquid.

Before I drank, I toasted to the old dim painting hanging above the bar: a ruddy, mustachioed man who wore a barkeep's apron and an unreadable expression. Everyone just called him The Proprietor. Supposedly he was the man who made the bar, or the first owner of The Broken Hourglass or any variation depending on who was telling the story. Tales flowed as freely as the booze, but were generally cheaper. The constant one was that no one had ever shorted the house—that rumored rule had stood for as long as The Broken Hourglass had.

I took a swallow. The aged bourbon was smooth, but there was a smokiness I couldn't place. Another sip and the heat became evident, if not identifiable. Maxine was about to flit by the table, and I raised my hand to flag her down.

"Another round, Mister St. Clair? Really warms ya up, don't it?" she chattered as she started back to the bar.

"Not yet, can't seem to place—"

She spun on her heel and said, "Absolutely, I have some matches, oops, butterfingers, jeez!" as a box of matches spilled on the table. She leaned over me as she gathered them, and whispered, "Ashes of Goody Alesworth — on the stake, 1697."

Taking a quick peek at The Proprietor's portrait over the bar, a small smile quirked one corner of her mouth, and as soon as the matches were back in the box, she said loudly, "Can you believe a little cinnamon can give that kind of bite, Mister St. Clair? Now don't be tellin' everybody Beau's secrets!" as she shot off again.

And that, ladies and gentlemen, is why The Broken Hourglass is a watering hole exceptionale. This was going to cost me, but when it came to booze or broads, the bank of St. Clair was always open.

The lights dimmed. The room's mood shifted as a single spot appeared on the small stage. When Kitty Cantrell came on, the crowd hushed and even the constant cocktail shaker was silenced.

She slid into the spotlight as intimately as it if were a hot bath. The light glittered off the sequins that spilled down the front of her dress. A slow smile spread across her face and a slight shiver moved over her bare caramel-colored shoulders. She looked out into the crowd, eyes flecked with the colors of a fading sun.

Taking a moment, she picked the lone glass up off the small stool and took a sip of her ever-present Pink Lady (though Maxine mentioned once, it smelled of copper and cream). She tilted the drink towards Lamentation, and mouthed, "It was dreamy." He started a slow tinkling lead into "Dream a Little Dream of Me."

Kitty worked it into a sultry torch song for each man in the room, and for him alone. Which is why I found the sudden tugging at my arm so damn irksome.

"St. Clair, old boy, didn't think I'd find you anywhere," said the distraction. "You don't mind if I join you, do you old friend?"

Sliding into the chair opposite me was none other than the bespectacled Benjamin Archibald. So terribly British, so terribly smart, and always so terribly "Benny," which is why I tried to be nonchalant, as I made sure I still had my wallet. His natty navy blue suit was a bit rumpled and his upper lip had a sheen of sweat.

"Quite a day, quite a day, if I do so say," he said as he held up two fingers to Maxine and pointed to what was now "our" table.

"Really, Benny?" I asked, eyes back on the stage. "Tough day in the stacks?" Benny was a whiz at the parchment and provenance game, knowing something about everything, and always looking to make little lucre.

"Oh no, old boy, been doing a bit of moonlighting, you know. Been helping out El-Roque. Bit of a warren, his place is."

"Didn't think he was still in the game," I said.

In his day, El-Roque the Arabian antiquarian was the man to see. Almost every upscale enclave or midtown museum had one of his finds. Now rumor had it he had a serious grudge against Howard Carter and his diggers. No one likes competition, least of all, archeological acquisitionists.

"That's just it, St. Clair, the old sands are starting to shift, if you know what I mean," he replied, tapping his index finger to his temple. A bit of smugness crept back into his sweaty countenance. "Which is why he's hired yours truly to help catalog his considerable collection."

Huh, "Benny the Brain" working in the inner sanctum of El-Roque? I'd have bet booze would be legal again before that happened.

"BZZZ! BZZZ! BZZZ!" The alarm sounded, breaking my thoughts. "BZZZ! BZZZ! BZZZ!"

The place broke into a hurried but practiced routine. Drinks disappeared, coffee and Cubans were passed out, and a number of hardbound books were placed around.

Turk's huge hand drew back the curtain and O'Malley, the neighborhood beat cop stepped in. His familiar brogue rang out.

"Now why is it when I get a report of..." he flipped open a small notebook, "'a bookworm bein' chased by a naked albino,' I am not in the least surprised that he is seen runnin' down this particular alley?"

My head turned quickly to what now was an empty chair across from me. A quick sweep of the room showed no sign of Benny.

"Now officer, surely, you don't think—" asked Kitty from the stage, a small poetry volume now in place of her drink.

"Apologies, for interruptin' your performance, Miss Kitty," he replied, touching his cap. "But I have to at least take a look around this, ahem, 'Literary social club.'"

8

O'Malley walked slowly through while Kitty did a reading of "Fire and Ice" that was light on the second part. It gave me a moment to think about why Benny looked like he'd just run the quarter mile. And where the hell was the "naked albino?"

Kitty finished up the Frost to laughter and applause. When O'Malley reached for the curtain that led to the rear, Lamentation started up at the piano.

"Now, officer, surely this room o' reprobates and roundheads ca'na do this song justice?" he began the opening bars of "Too-Ra-Loo-Ra–Loo-Ral."

O'Malley, to his credit, had a look on his face that said he knew he was being snookered. However, his pride at being a child soloist at All Souls Cathedral, as he was fond of telling folks on his beat, wouldn't let him pass this by. He got to about the second chorus of "Ral" before a scream erupted from the back, shattering the Celtic charm.

Benny's voice rang out, "No, no, please, no!" He scrambled out, wrapped in panic and the velvet curtain. He was trying to make it to the front door when his pursuer burst from backstage.

Now, the "naked albino" made sense.

Half human, half-canine, all fish-belly white, the ghul tore at the fabric and was stunned by the light and the noise. Ghuls under the best of circumstances are hard on the eyes. This one in a rotting loincloth, fierce and fever-eyed, driven half-mad by the city was a particularly nasty number.

The place went crazy—screams, curses, an explosion of movement. O'Malley reacted quickly with a right hook that he actually landed. The hairless beast twisted and sprang at him and down they went in a tumble of brogue and snarl.

Across the way, Vincent "Vicious" Halley moved with his

notorious speed. He may have been an unrepentant killer, but Ma Halley had raised him right. While standing, one hand swept the blonde doxy unceremoniously to the floor behind him, as the other flicked open a wicked looking blade. His two leg breakers got up: one sticking close and one going to take care of whatever was alarming their boss. I seriously doubted that any goon was going to be able to stop a ghul.

Officer O'Malley was holding his own, but he didn't know how durable his undead dance partner was. He had the right balance of insularity and indifference to keep this place quiet. Not to mention a dead copper was trouble in anybody's book. No sense letting this sanctuary for the sinful get shuttered. I reached inside my inner coat pocket to grab my "leveler," a set of silver knuckles with a little reliquary wallop inside.

Imagine my surprise when I grabbed something else instead. It was a tiny carved statue, obsidian, a man's body with a jackal's head, adorned with gold and tiny gems. Confused, I dropped it back in my coat and dug out the knuckles. As I edged towards the fight, all of a sudden everything clicked.

"Benny, you son of a—"

I caught the backswing from Halley's goon as he tried to brain the ghul with a chair. The knuckledusters flew through the air, clattering onto the small stage.

"Ah got it, Mistah St. Clairah!" yelled Beau. The southern spirit blinked out from behind the bar and reappeared in front of the stage. Kitty had already backed out of the blinding spotlight, eyes narrowed and hands curling.

My head was still ringing from catching that chair across the chin. "Uhhnn, Beau, don't," I mumbled. Too little, too late. My warning was drowned out by his terrible scream. Beau's form flickered like a bad bulb. The spectral hand he'd used to grab at the knuckles was shredded like crepe, blowing silently in an other-dimensional wind.

Kitty was backed up against the corner, eyes wide with fright, nerves strung taut. Her teeth had become pointed and her eyes glowed a slight orange against her café-au-lait skin. A throaty growl replaced her usual silken tones and her irises narrowed into slits.

The ghul spun at the noise, lunging toward the stage. It had obviously never worked in showbiz. Stars don't like to share the spotlight, and Kitty was no exception. The snarl that came from her had none of the sultriness of the starlet. That was a sound that used to keep the "marks" huddled in their caves. Cornered and at the end of her tether, Kitty sprang. The result was something I wish I could have sold tickets to.

"Halley!" I yelled over the din, and Vicious squinted at me. I motioned a fist towards the whirl of white flesh and evening gown. He tapped his other man and sent him in. Well trained or well paid, the muscle entered the fray. It wasn't pretty, but he bought me the time to get over to the stage and grab the silver knuckles.

Giving a wide berth to the still flickering Beau, I tried to clear my head and time my entrance into this little dance. Halley's second boy was a momentary distraction at best. The poor sap was hopelessly outclassed. He must have done something good in a past life, 'cause he got in a couple of licks and then sailed across the room with a thud, instead of being cut to ribbons.

Kitty was prowling around now, barely holding onto her humanity, with fur and fang coming to the surface. The ghul was trying to watch her and any other movement when a flickering form blinked in behind it. Beau latched his good arm around the thing's neck. I don't know who was more surprised, the ghul or me. God bless the glorious dead.

"Mistah St. Clairah, if you would?" he yelled, as he struggled, not only to hold on, but also to hold his ghostly form together.

I, of course, had only hesitated to give Beau his moment in the sun. Throwing all of my weight into the punch, I clocked the ghul right in the jaw. Its head snapped back, there was a thunderclap and what felt like stepping onto the third rail. Beau had vanished, the ghul was down, and I flew back into a heap.

Being somewhat used to the constant ringing in my head, I recovered faster than the rest. The ghul had a scorch mark on its face, and wasn't moving, but I probably only bought Benny until sundown the next night. The sooner we got the statue and the ghul out of here, the better.

Since I was one of the only things moving in the place, I helped myself to a drink and tried to think. Lamentation staggered over from the piano and helped himself to a whiskey.

"Sweet mother o' night, look at this place." he muttered. I had seen worse, but usually I slipped away before the dust cleared. We clinked glasses and knocked back the drinks, then something caught Lamentation's eye.

"Ya ready for some more good news, St. Clair?"

"What now?"

"The eyes o' that charming portrait o'er the bar just shifted ta black. Ya'd better sit down," he said as he pushed me into a nearby chair. "That usually means a private word, in three, two, one."

The voice that then filled my head made Turk sound like a

whispering soprano. "Your man has accrued debts, and you have waylaid the collector. This is a square house, would you be assuming his debts?"

"My man?" My head swam as I found my voice, "Benny, Benny's debts?" I stammered. "I can't begin to think what he owes."

"Then the doorman will assure that he will not flee from El-Roque's next agent."

I'd seen Turk's handiwork before; it was reported as a trampling by a team of horses. Benny was a worm, but he was a useful worm, and he'd done a couple of decent turns for yours truly.

"Why not let me collect, just for tonight's debts? El-Roque's ghul did bust up your place. That way El-Roque'll get his pound of flesh and you don't look like a pushover. Anything outside between Benny and him is just that."

There was a silence and I waited to join the choir eternal.

"The night's receipts will be lacking," the voice threatened.

I winced. Benny's tabs would have to be paid and better me than management. I took a breath and made my peace with it.

"I ... I'll make sure he evens the till."

"See that you do." And with that, I was snapped back to the here and now.

"Ya be wantin' some help trussin' up that corpse eater?" Lamentation spat as my focus returned.

"Much obliged."

"Just keep those accursed knuckles away from me, and ya got yerself a deal."

"Not you, too?"

"Hah, did ya think it was but the wee people that left the

isle, St. Clair?"

"D'ja know there was going to be trouble?"

"Do I look Greek? I'm a banshee, not a bloody oracle! But no one's leaving the mortal coil, at least not in here tonight," he said as he looked over the unmoving forms of the cop and the customers.

Dragging the ghul into the back, using an old tarp and some rope, we "wrapped it well enough to make a fishmonger proud," Lamentation declared.

Even while doing that, I was thinking about The Proprietor, and the painting still swam in my vision. He and El-Roque apparently bowled in the same league. I could ruminate about the movers and shakers later. I sighed because now I had to introduce someone to the bar's namesake.

I found my dear friend Benny, cowering behind an overturned table and feigning unconsciousness. I ever so gently helped him up by his lapels and then over to the bar.

"Now, now, Saint, St. Clair," Benny stammered. "Remember the docks, an-an-and those Dagonites."

I sighed. The Dagonites. He never lets me forget about the Dagonites.

"Fine, Benny. But you know I should just hand you over to El-Roque." I looked over the damage to the place, the scuffed up singer, and the unconscious cop. I walked behind the bar, grabbed the small plain box in a niche by the cash register, and placed it next to him.

"This was dumb, especially for a smart guy like you. And it's gonna cost you to make it right. Hell, Benny, I don't even know if this'll clear the board, but it'll give you a little breathing room."

I took the small timer out of the box, and it didn't look like much. The truly dangerous stuff never did. Besides, this one had cracked glass and barely any sand left at the bottom.

Benny looked fish-eyed when I brought it out, and then relieved. The dope.

"Like any theft you're pinched for, this one's gonna cost you time," I said.

"Oh, very droll, very droll indeed." The relief brought back the old Benny. "Reparations for a new egg timer? Done!" he called out with wavering bravado.

I chanced a look behind him into the mirror and vaguely saw the misty form of Beau floating in the glass. He looked away out of respect, a ghost who was haunted by what I was about to do to someone I called a friend.

I grabbed Benny's left hand, shoved the tiny timepiece into it and closed my fists around his hand. I ground the jagged edges into his palm. He gasped at the cuts, and then his voice left him as the timer started.

The lights dimmed in the place and our hands quaked, but I didn't dare let go. Benny'd made his bed and now he was going to have to lie in it. He became pale and drawn. His legs shook and buckled. His eyes rolled back and I didn't release his hand until he was on the floor and the only thing holding him up was me.

Carefully opening my hands, I saw the brilliant glow of the timer now filled with motes of light. I removed it from Benny's palm and let him fall to the floor completely.

Amazing. The lights were hypnotic.

I carefully poured them into the tiny vials in the timer's box. One I filled only one-fourth of the way: for the loss of the night's take, and placed it into a small slot in the bar. Three more vials I filled completely and placed them into my knotted up pocket square along with the statue.

I went in back and tucked the beggar's purse into the ghul "Catch of the Day" package. When night fell, the foul thing would scurry back to El-Roque like some undead homing pigeon, now that it had its prize.

Benny looked like hell, breath ragged and eyes unfocused. I reached down and took out his billfold. Acquiring enough for a generous donation for O'Malley's "widows and orphans fund" and a new frock for the feral femme, I tossed it back onto his chest.

"St. Clair, what the bloody hell?" he asked, in between heaving gasps.

"Benny, I just saved your life by taking it from you. Three years for theft, and three months for disturbing the peace." My voice sounded hard even to me. "Some of those aches and pains aren't going to go away anytime soon. Had to skim it off the top, Benny, the good years. Take what you've got left in your wallet and your soul and get the hell outta town before nightfall."

A range of emotions passed over his face, but the fallback of blueblood bluster stuck. "Good, good show, old boy." He shakily stood, and turned to preen himself with a quavering hand in the mirror. "The Nile is lovely this time of year and that Carter fellow may need some help with his newest dig."

Benny was always going to be Benny, never one to stumble over scruples, nor bodies, as he gingerly stepped over the now-waking crowd. When he got to the curtain, he paused.

"St. Clair?"

"We're good, Benny. Just watch yourself." A small smile came back to my face. "You're not as young as you used to be."

Chad Kroll is thrilled to have this opportunity. He has had a tenuous grasp on reality from a young age and is glad to have finally found a use for it. The author has been previously published in G-FAN, a magazine devoted to Godzilla and other kaiju, now in its 24th year of publication (#98, "Wake Up, Kalamazoo!"). This writing rat would like to thank the two oxen in his life who carry him along, and the Pandemonium Illiterati for their encouragement and entertainment. As the late, great Bela Lugosi once said: "Begin the brain transplant!"

The Lurker

Orin Kornblit

The creature lurked.

Then it skulked. When that didn't help, it tried creeping. Finally it gave up, squelched its way out of the bog, across the street and into the Jones' residence, found the elderly couple ensconced in their living room and promptly ate them.

The creature sat there for a while afterwards, trying to feel satisfied. Idly picking its teeth with one of Mrs. Jones' tibias, it flipped channels on the television that had so absorbed their attention.

Nothing on. Not a damned thing.

And the television had seemed so interesting from across the street too. With no sound and only partially discernible images visible from the bog, it had been a source of wonder and mystery. Now it was clear those feelings had been a product of the creature's own longings.

The creature splorched into the kitchen. Not much there either. Lots of cold, dead meat in the fridge. Nothing edible. It tried the basement. It only found the family cat, which went down swiftly but wasn't very satisfying. Too small and too hairy. Nothing like the fish it used to eat.

Those days were gone. Fish had become scarce. And the whale-songs, when they could be heard at all, were lamentations of longing and despair. The seas were nearly empty. The creature had been forced to try its luck along the coasts. Then the swamps. And now, finally, on land.

Land. It was nothing like the enveloping comfort of the sea. Even worse, every place the creature went felt the same. Dull. Monotonous.

The creature's stomach gurgled. It was still hungry. Sometimes the creature didn't know why it even bothered. What was it all for, anyway?

A more thorough search of the kitchen rewarded it with a pile of take-out menus. It ordered a pizza. Twenty-five minutes later the pie arrived, delivered by a pimply-faced teenager.

He was delicious. Even better than fish. Burping loudly, the creature tossed the pizza aside and settled into Mr. Jones' well-worn, plush leather recliner. Despite its now full belly, the creature's mood hadn't improved.

After digesting for an hour or so, it shook itself out of its funk and pushed the delivery boy's car into the bog. The creature glomped back to the house and slurphed from room to room in increasing despair.

It did a load of laundry, changed the light bulb in the bathroom that Mr. Jones had promised his wife he would fix a month ago and, in a last ditch effort to keep ennui at bay, emptied the dishwasher.

The creature was about ready to pack it in when it found the computer. It sat on a small desk, nearly hidden in a corner and covered in dust. A flimsy chair sat beside it, supporting a precariously balanced pile of unopened mail.

With a little experimentation, the creature managed to turn the neglected device on. A few tentative clicks later it found the internet and began exploring. The creature was fascinated. Here was a whole world, filled with conversations and discussions beyond anything in its experience.

It dragged the recliner over to the disused desk, tossing aside the plastic chair in a small whirlwind of urgent credit card offers and desperate discount circulars. The creature settled in amidst the scattered papers and read deep into the night.

The creature was still reading when the sun rose. It stopped long enough to sort the mail and pay the bills, effortlessly imitating Mrs. Jones' flowing cursive handwriting. It ate the postman when he came by, which might have been a mistake. Now it would have to squelch down to the mailbox at the corner once it was dark.

The creature went back to the computer. Too shy to dare posting its own words, it devoured page after page of thoughts and dreams, hopes and fears, petty complaints and noble aspirations.

The creature lurked.

Orin Kornblit likes to start his day with a hot cup of coffee and end it with a cold beer.

He has had an adventurous life, starting with a five-year

mission to boldly go where millions of science fiction fans had gone before. He's been to a galaxy far, far away, journeyed to the center of the Earth and traveled twenty-thousand leagues under the sea. He spent five years in deep space, at a port of call, a home away from home, for diplomats, hustlers, entrepreneurs and wanderers.

He's journeyed through the Mines of Moria, searched for a crystal shard, fell down a rabbit hole and munched on lembas bread while losing his marbles with the Mad Hatter. He's wandered in a labyrinth through dangers untold and hardships unnumbered, with his phaser set on stun and relying on the red settings of his trusty sonic screwdriver.

He's hitched a ride in a Tardis, coming prepared with his towel and Joo Janta 200 Super-Chromatic Peril Sensitive Sunglasses. He popped in for a quick pint at The White Hart before going as far back as the Hyborian Age and then forward to the dry, desolate planet of Arrakis and the Imperial Palace on Trantor.

None of his travels, however, can ever compare to the wonder and joy given him by his lovely wife and three beautiful children.

These days, Orin's life is quieter. He splits his time between working in healthcare and creating new adventures for others to enjoy.

Botanical Difficulties

Chris Howard

Still a bit weedy from the eleven-year journey from Earth, Research Fellow Huan Norr stepped off the curb two blocks from the Lassandra Worldport and a delivery vehicle hit him at high speed.

Huan had been squeezing his wallet open, thumbing through the ticket deck for the tab that would take him to Siddaq Reach when the delivery vehicle's low hood shoveled his legs out from under him. His body was thrown a few meters into the air above the street, sending his arms into a clockwise spiral, shoulders dislocated, his travel pack in emergency mode, clinging heavily to his suit.

Time slowed. Lassandra's air was thick. His gaze slid toward the vehicle, a blur of slick white molding, afternoon starlight papering the windshield in wide opaque sheets. Through one clear slice in the reflection Huan saw the driver's teeth, a double row of angry ivory, lips peeled back like a skull's.

A childish idea banged around the edge of his thoughts, something from the page notes in the visitor expectations doc, and he was thinking, *less grav here on Lassandra, maybe I'll bounce.* Huan hit the pavement hard. Bones crumbled, organs sloshed and compressed, his skull felt as if it was in a couple of pieces, cupping his brain like a wad of wet clay in a box of broken pottery. Huan's travel pack hugged him lovingly, remain-with-passenger enabled.

Sir Philip is going to be so disappointed.

≪⑤

"Mr. Norr? Huan Norr? Of Cambridge, England, Earth?"

The room rocked slowly like a boat in a calm. Huan opened his mouth, and his breath hit something hard that stood a few centimeters off his face, turning each exhale back to eddy warmly around his cheeks. The slow rocking came from the motion of his chest rising and falling. He remembered a woman's voice, calling his name, then the hiss of released pressure and the seals of the surgery case coming loose. Huan opened his eyes, and they went wide on their own, his face moving reflexively, startled, seconds too late.

"Yes?" His voice was crusty, dry and unused, as if he hadn't spoken in days. He sat up slowly, braced on his elbows.

"Please stand, sir," she said politely, soft practiced edges in her tone.

Huan blinked and put some effort into keeping his sight under control, trying to find her eyes, or at least hold his focus on her face, but his gaze slipped down her jawline, along a slender line of gold jewelry at her throat to a pink badge pinned to the stiff white collar of her uniform. Post-Surgery Care, Technician

Benecka.

What sort of name was that? Trying to think back on the Lassandra cultural handbook. Large population from São Paulo here, significant numbers from central Africa, a smaller set from a city in the American mid-west, Lafayette, Indiana, he thought—a bunch of Purdue grads caught up in the colonial spirit of the time.

Benecka had her hair pulled into a tail at the back. Her face was a fit combination of rounded edges and planes, warm brown skin with freckles on her nose, a perfect circular mole at the apex of her arched right eyebrow, and a tiny four-petal flower tattoo marking the joint of her jawbone. Her eyes were unusual. They held Huan's for a moment, purple facets with tiny brown flecks, amethyst and autumn leaves.

"One foot at a time, Mr. Norr."

A flower's scent distracted him, sweet, with a hint of soft citrus.

Huan twisted around, looking for the source as he pulled his knees up and threw his feet over the flexible edge of the case. He pushed off with his hands and landed unsteadily on the tiles. Benecka shook her head, disapproving, and caught him by the shoulders.

"They're fresh," she said, hastily covering a reproach when she saw him glance back at the vivid orange blossoms in a vase on a corner wall ledge. "MedCenter puts those in every in-coming's room."

"Do they?" he asked and looked around the pale green cube with a new eye, stopping on the view through the windows. The horizon cut the scene in equal parts, cloudy sky and lush green and fuchsia forest roof. The distant view didn't hide the fact that some of the plant life grew at odd angles, not drawn toward Lassandra's star.

Sir Philip was right. My kind of world.

Benecka gave his shoulders a quick squeeze to remind him to stand on his own, and turned to pull out a set of hospital garments from the closet.

He dressed while she directed two more techs to remove the surgical case, then she waved him back in bed, came around, and tied him to the mattress by a thin flexible strap that led from his left wrist to a holdfast on the side.

Huan stared at the centimeter-wide binding that squeezed gently against his skin, some sort of smart material that expanded and contracted with his movement. He still felt the residuals from surgery, and it gave him a detached view of the action around him, made him more curious than angry.

"What's this for?" He pulled on it to gauge its strength then yanked hard, using his body's weight, lifting the mattress.

Benecka made one eyebrow jump, amused. "A light restraint, not meant to hold you back, but you'd look silly dragging your mattress behind you."

Huan drew a breath, let his thoughts find some order, directing them gently toward the correct name for the police. *Lassandra Enforcement, something like that?*

Benecka read the look and said, "LEX wants to talk to you about yesterday's accident."

He was about to ask what that meant, but she straightened suddenly, her gaze wandering off to the wall above his head, listening to some internal comm gear. "You have a visitor, a Mr. Musni. A bakery owner." Her mouth went crooked, not quite a smile. "Perhaps someone's sent you cookies?"

He shook his head automatically. *Sir Philip Wallace isn't a cookie person.*

Benecka eyed Mr. Musni as they passed each other at the doorway, but tilted her head in automatic greeting. The baker returned something less than cordial.

Musni went straight for him, bloodshot eyes blinking and narrowing as he leaned in to study his face. Huan smiled reservedly and dropped his gaze to the baker's hands. Where were the cookies?

Maybe there was a mistake? Musni flexed the fingers on one hand, tightening each into a fist, then dug around and pulled the other hand from his jacket pocket with a handgun. "Even up time, Mr. Norr." He laughed suddenly—starting with a chuckle he couldn't hold in, and then into real laughter as if someone had told an especially funny joke.

Terribly funny.

"What do you want?" Looking at the gun, Huan's voice came out thin, gasping the words. Scariest damned baker he had ever met.

"You, Mr. Norr, in pieces that can't be put back together, Mr. Norr." Musni kept saying his name. The baker barked another laugh. "It's fitting. 'Nor' is the name of a common snail-like creature here, a nasty pest that gardeners poison. Wholesale slaughter of Nors is widespread on Lassandra." Musni spat out the last line and raised his gun, aiming at his target's face.

Huan couldn't move—except to pull the restraint tight against his left wrist. And then parts of the hospital room unfolded, sections of the far wall splitting open.

The span of a single second stretched out to some unknowable horizon, everything going slow, all human intention throttled down to a snail's pace. And the machines took over at nanosecond speeds. A battery of stunners dropped from ceiling panels, swung to Musni, sighted and fired. The baker went rigid, lost his gun in the disruption, and sagged along the wall to the floor, his eyes rolling up behind half opened lids.

Benecka was back. She skidded against the doorframe, out of breath. "Mr. Norr?"

Her voice released the lock on his muscles.

Huan gasped out the words, "You have guns in the ceiling?"

She stepped in cautiously, waving to the weaponry above them. "Just in these post-op rooms. For patient's under LEX hold."

"HOLD!"

Huan jumped in shock, snapping the restraint tight as four commandos stormed in. Two went to the windows, necks craning to study the MedCenter grounds. One remained at the door, facing the hall. The last holstered a handgun and bowed to Benecka, smiling like an old friend. She returned the smile, leaning in to take his forearm in one hand, gazes locked while she passed along information—probably patient history and security details.

He gave her a slight nod of his head. "Always pleased to see you, technician."

His gaze shot briefly to one of the window guards, passing a command to clean up Mr. Musni. He bent down and spent a moment studying the gun Musni had pulled, and then he looked at Huan, his smile remaining.

He might have been a descendant of the African spacefarers, speaking English with an accent vaguely French—but that didn't mean much anymore. It was just as likely that one or both of his parents had been Purdue students, raised in Indiana. His skin was the color of a cup of long-steeped tea with fine lines of age starting at the corners of his eyes and mouth. No taller than Benecka in his combat boots, he was broader, muscular, and went halfway to crushing Huan's hand in a shake.

"Good to have you in one piece, Mr. Huan Norr. You were an absolute humpty when they brought you in." He tipped his head to Benecka. "Finest treatment services on Lassandra right here in the Worldport. I'm told seven hours in surgery before they had you glued back together." He let out a short high whistle, clearly amazed.

"I seem to be. My strength has returned." Huan rubbed his chin and leaned over to look at the gray stripes on the uniform's shoulder, wondering at his rank. "Although, it's a bit awkward to have someone—a baker of all things—want to kill me."

The soldier noticed his glance at his sleeve. "Sergeant. Sergeant Nesham." The sergeant gestured to the limp body on the floor. "Mr. Musni was operating the vehicle that hit you."

Sergeant Nesham gave Huan a slight smiling nod at what he saw in his face, and then turned to Benecka. "Please give me a few moments with Mr. Norr."

The rest of the security team also left, one pushing Musni out on a gurney.

Nesham swung back, smile gone, just sharp calculating eyes. He leaned forward. "Did Musni say anything to you?"

Huan felt warm, embarrassed about the weird exchange with the baker. His face clearly showed it, and the Sergeant ratcheted up the seriousness in his stare. Nesham gestured for him to speak.

"He laughed at me. He said I shared my family name with a snail that Lassandran gardeners regularly exterminate."

"Different spelling. What else?"

"Nothing. He just pulled the gun ... and laughed about my name. I only knew his name because the technician told me."

Nesham glanced at the ceiling thoughtfully, tilting his head as if listening to something only he could hear. "MedCenter scanned Musni coming through the front door."

"Don't they scan for weaponry?"

Nodding, the sergeant waved a hand at the open tiles and stunners, made a wider sweeping gesture to indicate the entire hospital building. "That's worrying. It's normal. Musni walked right in through the front doors, carrying something out of the ordinary, not picked up by any scans. Stuff's priced way out of his range."

"And bakers usually carry arms here on Lassandra?"

Nesham smiled. "This one did. Musni's specialty is wedding cakes and custom dining services for ... special customers. Even if some of his clients aren't of the highest quality, Musni has a healthy rep." Nesham frowned, his gaze drifting away, toward the windows and strange bent trees along the horizon. "Well, he *did*. Then you showed up."

The sergeant left two of his commandos to guard the room, one positioned against the window, the other at the door, weapons out, pointed at the floor. Benecka returned twice to check on him, the last time to tell him that Sergeant Nesham was questioning the baker, and would be back tomorrow for a follow-up.

The evening slipped by, and Huan remained tied to his mattress. He couldn't sleep, and sat up late, flipping through some churnpaper, reading back-issues of the *Journal of Aquatic Xenobotany*, going through the one that contained Wallace's, "Seasonal growth of the two Laviolanis sp. in Siddaq Peninsula on Lassandra." It was still under review when Huan had left Earth, although Wallace shot him a pre-press copy to read along the way.

"Sir Philip Wallace," He whispered, trying to keep the reverence out of his voice. He let the journal hardcopy fall on his chest and closed his eyes.

Huan woke to the sound of a sloppy wet thump against the windows, and shot up in bed. A dark smear of motion pulled his focus around, one of Nesham's commandos pointing at him with a gloved hand. He shouted, "DOWN!" but the soldier was only halfway through the one syllable when the limpets blew, throwing high-velocity angles of window into the room.

Seven hours of surgery and some rest had done wonders for his reflexes. Huan heaved his body away from the blast. The mattress followed on its leash, shielding him for the most part. He landed face down on the floor.

Groaning against the cold tiles, it seemed several seconds before the window shards finished carving up the inside of his hospital room, and several more for the sound of falling wall board, clothes hangers and pieces of the closet door to come to rest.

There was a pause of silence and then the light crunch of boots on debris and broken windowpanes. More ceiling panels dropped, stunners ranged and fired, and the intruder went down in the rubble.

"Not another baker?" Huan cried, a shallow madness seizing him as a tech named Mauro snipped the restraint and pulled him from the ruins of his room.

A shiver ran through his body, fear sloshing up against the inside of his head, mounting and rolling back to his feet. He rocked unsteadily and followed Mauro down the hall. He barely noticed the yellow crisis strobes and beeping tones from monitors up and down the post-op wing.

Mauro strode ahead to find a place for him, and Huan, still unsteady, slammed rudely into a heavyset blond man coming the other way, body gown and face mask up for surgery.

"I am so sorry." Huan's hands came up shaking. "I don't know —"

"No, please, the fault is mine." The man shook his head dizzily, eyes wide, apologetic. "I wasn't paying attention either. Careful with this."

Green-gloved fingers swung into view like a magician's trick, gingerly holding a sprig of some thorny plant. Huan took it, immediately intrigued by any kind of flora, but his interest quickly dropped as the thorns went through his skin and made a bloody mess of his fingers. The doctor or whatever he was in the mask and gown bent to retrieve a stack of books Huan had knocked from his arms. The man thanked him, and plucked the sprig of thorny plant from him.

Huan wiped his hands on his hospital pajamas, the light material already streaked with dust from the wallboard and speckled in what may have been blood from one of the commandos.

Mauro returned, having made some temporary arrangements, led Huan to a chair in a room at the end of the wing, and left him.

"You ain't hammered are you?"

Huan looked up at unshaven features, creases deepening around the corners of a man's mouth as he pulled his face into an angry knot, white eyebrows jutting militaristically, hands curled into fists.

"No." Huan wasn't level on his feet, but no reason to jump to conclusions. "Someone just tried to kill me."

"Oh." The double-room's only occupant nodded. "In that case, Carl Deprato." He waved congenially, and then flipped one thumb at the other bed, neatly wrapped, ready for a patient. "We bunking together now?"

Deprato had the bed by the window, which was fine by Huan. "I'm not sure. I think the tech brought me here to sit down while they clean up my room."

"You got a name?"

He started, nodding regretfully. "Sorry. The blast knocked my manners crooked. Huan Norr. Pleasure to meet you, Carl."

"Huan? You from Earth?"

He nodded, rubbing his eyes. The little nubs of thorn bites on his fingers were rough on his lids. "From the Philippines, Iraq, most recently from England."

"What brings you out to Lassandra?"

Huan was too tired to shake Carl off. "Plant studies. Non-phototropic mechanisms. I'm a student of Sir Philip Wallace."

He felt the temp drop in the room. After a long pause Deprato asked, "What's non-phototropic?"

"You know, the way plants bend toward light? Well, some don't. They bend toward ... something else."

Deprato shook his head. "I was born here."

Botanist mode kicked in. "Phototropism in Earth plants is the result of the regulated distribution of the hormone auxin that weighs down the stems and leaves on the side opposite the sun, bending the plant in order to maximize the reception of incident light."

"You going to study the Laviolas then?"

Everybody does. Huan nodded. That part wasn't a secret. They were tourist traps anyway. You couldn't come to Lassandra and not see at least one of the six remaining Laviola species. And for a botanist, they were Mecca.

He didn't need to know that so much of the Lassandran botanical life was drawn to the gigantic plant-like structures of the Laviolanis species, rather than the star's own light. Sir Philip thought he knew why, and Huan was Sir Philip's friend and student, handpicked for the next great advancement in the botanical sciences, sent across the stars to make the discovery, to make the sacrifice. He felt a spark of daring flare up inside him. Carl looked old enough, and Huan had picked up an obvious animosity toward his teacher. "What can you tell me of Sir Philip's work when he was here?"

Deprato snorted at the title. "Knighted, eh?"

"Yeah, it's an English thing. Two years before I left Earth." He ticked the numbers off in his head. "Almost thirteen years ago, when he went virtual, just after he was awarded the post of Professor of Botany at Cambridge."

"We don't get regular news from Earth, just the big stuff, costs too much, and there's still a sixteen day lag on that. We don't have real full-time virtual here yet, just the games and transients. Not enough wealth on Lassandra for fulltime virtual, not even the ORCs have enough to import the tech. We live and die physical. Same as it's always been. Oh, and Sir Philip left my father to die. The grief sucked the life from my mother. My father's slow madness drained her spirit. She died before I was twenty."

Silence in the room, nothing but the tick of the alert lights pulsing down the hall.

Then Huan started breathing again. "I'm ... I'm sorry," He whispered automatically, eyes on the tiles, his head suddenly becoming too heavy to lift.

"It was a long time ago." A sharp edge slid into Deprato's voice. "You aren't going to ask how?"

Of course, it suddenly gnawed at him. He didn't want to know. "Sir Philip's a very ... driven man."

"He went offworld seventy years ago, and left his students to die, torn, piece by piece, feeding the Laviola at Siddaq. They were all tagged, and Sir Philip Wallace let them, encouraged them to become part of its life-cycle, told them it was the only way we'd be able to understand how the Laviola works. He said 'We' and then let *them* die. Wallace got away clean, sneaking off Lassandra like a fucking yurn-rodent."

He wouldn't do that. Huan started down the defensive path, and pulled up quickly, connections from Carl's story dropping into place. "Your mother wasn't a student?"

"She was. She escaped the Lavi. Became un-tagged."

Huan choked on the surprise. "I didn't know that was possible."

Carl Deprato gave him a doubtful squint. "The hammers left her alone."

Huan leaned back. "Hammers?"

"You playing stupid, scholar boy?"

He shook his head.

"Your mother?" Benecka asked sharply from the door. They both swung to her. "She gave birth to you, Mr. Deprato. That's why."

Benecka tossed the *Journal of Aquatic Xenobotany* to Huan accusingly. She had picked it out of the ruins of his hospital room. "A botanist? You're here to study the Laviolanis?" She cut off the upswing of his nod with, "What the fuck could you possibly know about it?" She gestured impatiently.

Her sharp reaction scared him. He stuttered a little, gathering words. *Just answer the question.* "I know the plant—"

"It kills people, takes their spirit. It's much more than a plant and you know it, Norr." She pointed at the journal.

Wallace had hinted at local antagonism, but he hadn't expected every other person on Lassandra to be familiar with the Laviola lifecycle or Wallace's work—or part of some anti-Wallace conspiracy.

"I know it can grow to the size of a small city, there's only six of them on the planet, it chemically tags its victims, it acts as a breeding farm for a Lassandran chiropteran."

"The bats are called 'hammers' here."

"Ah." He nodded, getting Carl's first question—"hammered". He had heard the term before, but it was slang, and certainly didn't appear in the peer-reviewed press. "They obtain food for the Laviolanis, becoming its couriers. The plant enslaves the animals through addiction. The hammers have sophisticated homing processes. The Laviola injects a trace scent into humans —tags them, and the bats attack using a variety of methods, some of them very sophisticated for perceptual-level animals." Huan only paused for a breath, on a roll with his delivery. "Wallace says there's no range limit. The hammers will find you wherever you try to hide. They steal pieces of the tagged person, biting the skin, drawing blood, taking square centimeter portions at a time— approximately. The hammer returns to its source Laviolanis, offering the piece of you in exchange for its fix. Hammers breed, and their young are raised into addiction."

Nothing new here.

"Did you know the hammers don't attack if you peaceably allow them to take what they've come for? You didn't know the Laviola won't tag a woman who's pregnant?"

Benecka pulled him into her dark purple angry gaze. He felt his mouth sag open, and didn't do anything to stop it. This is what drove Sir Philip on. He tried to shrug, but couldn't get his muscles to respond in the right order. He gave up. "How does it know?" He breathed the words.

"Your job, not mine. Did you know that time slows to a crawl for the afflicted, but to the outside, it seems a wasting death, the worst form of punishment, harried by the bats who steal your flesh and blood to feed its master, the Lavi that bred it. Tagged ones go mad with nightmares, sensory displacement, waking dreams, visions. Mentally they're doomed. Unless you're female and able to bring a child to term, there's no coming out of it, and once you're infected—tagged—LEX won't let you offworld. A permanent quarantine on Lassandra."

Who is she? He tilted his head a little to get a better look. "Your tattoo?"

Her eyes narrowed. She swiveled her head, showing him her jaw and the little four-petal flower inked there. "I have a six-year-old son. I'm the only practicing tech at MedCenter with tagged patient care duties. There are only seven on the planet who want to get into it. Not a popular line of work."

The number seven cut through the web of thoughts building in Huan's head. "There used to be seven Laviolanis."

"The second wave colonists nuked one. We've always known there was something dangerous about them."

He knew the story—as fairly shallow history. He was just hoping Benecka would fill in some gaps.

Huan leaned back in the chair, pulled in a long breath and let it out, suddenly wondering if his teacher, Sir Philip Wallace, had betrayed him, sending him to Lassandra to become tagged by the Laviola at Siddaq Reach. If it meant his death, why would he do that ... *and to me, most devout, his greatest student?*

Carl stared out the window at the dawn. Benecka gripped the doorframe, and bent backward into the hall to follow some activity outside the room.

"Norr?"

He looked up, blinking. "What?"

"They ID'd the window-blowing intruder. It's the bride."

He gave her a blank stare.

"Nesham's here. C'mon. He'll tell you all about it."

Huan nodded to Carl on the way out, trying for friendliness, but it ended up cold. Benecka left him in a small conference room with Sergeant Nesham.

"Her name's Zona Spohnholtz."

Huan shook his head. "Never heard of her."

"You wouldn't. She just married the eldest Azzarito son." Nesham flipped up an image of a blond muscular man in an expensive suit, clean-shaven, eyes startling gray. "The ceremony was the day before yesterday, the day you arrived on Lassandra. Azzarito's one of the ORCs."

Huan Norr gave him his best one-raised-eyebrow-questioning-stare. "He doesn't look like the ones I'm familiar with." He had read the books, played the immersives. It had been a while, but orcs were something out of stories, not real, and even if they were, they didn't seem the sort that wore business suits.

"Syndicate, organized crime, bad guys. Azzarito plays right at the edge. And my guess's he's blaming you for disrupting his wedding. You know, it's supposed to be the happiest day of your life?"

Huan felt cold. "Me?"

Nesham shook his head. "The baker, Musni, was on his way to the ceremony, bringing the cake and four hundred confections. Not only did you hold him up, and prevent him from getting to the wedding on time, the cake didn't fare well. Plastered all over the back wall of his delivery car."

"Oh."

"Musni wants you dead. I suspect he's hired a backup in case he failed to kill you. So, that's another one you have to watch for. Musni apparently lost a lot of money on the deal. Zona wants you dead. You ruined her wedding. Azzarito wants you dead. You made his new wife cry. You're not a very popular man, Mr. Norr."

That's when the suffocating nightmares started. Huan gagged, rubbing his throat, and hit the floor.

✖

Huan Norr woke shaking, feverish, haunted by a continuous sensory stream that seeped into the corners of his mind. It touched every cell in his body, a cold, dark, drifting motion, sleep from which he couldn't wake, cables jacked into his skin, feeding the body, keeping it alive but suspended, outbound tubes brought his insides to the things that fed off his body, things with teeth.

"You're tagged."

He sat up on his elbows, shaking off grogginess. "What?"

Benecka stood at the foot of the bed, glaring at him as if it was his fault.

Huan tried to shake off the nightmare. "How?"

"You didn't come in tagged. You wouldn't have gone through surgery without it showing up. You've only been here three damn days!"

"I haven't been anywhere near a Laviola. I haven't been outside the hospital yet!"

"You have tickets to Siddaq in your wallet."

He gestured in front of her, as if evidence had been

39

presented. "Unused."

She nodded, waved away defeat, and tried a different line of attack. "You follow that fool, Wallace."

"A visionary," said Huan.

"Murderer."

"You don't know him. His students would follow him to the end of the universe."

"Messianic murderer, then."

He shook his head, despair in his voice. "I know him, maybe better than anyone ever has."

"What does that make you then?"

Huan Norr made fists when his hands started shaking.

Benecka answered before he could. "A fool."

The visions returned, a wave of force and cold fluid through his body, eyelids shuddering, a sea of solid darkness the folded in around him, icy against his face, and just a glimmer of light coming from somewhere above. He couldn't move. He fought the prison, drove every drop of strength into bending one finger—even the smallest, directing an eyelid to tremble. Nothing, just an inert anger.

He spent four days in the Worldport MedCenter infectious disease ward, quarantined, under full watch, and then the medical team and technician Benecka signed his release agreement.

She found him on the vista deck, staring out at the stretch of gold and fuchsia foliage to the horizon, rising here and there in clumps, flows of irregular branches at the base of blue and stone gray concrete towers, soft folds of forest showing where it followed the planet's terrain—and every leaf and blade and petal in view, a world full of them, grew to tilt and twist to face the flowering Laviola that rose in authority a thousand kilometers beyond the horizon along Siddaq Reach, a single plant as mysterious as it was monstrous, spiked glory and long shadows, with wide curls of blood red flowing from calyx to the floor like a conqueror's trophy banners.

Huan didn't turn around when Benecka cleared her throat, but she saw the quick tightening in his shoulders.

She said, "Keep a journal, but don't keep it to yourself."

He nodded at first, as if he barely heard her, then slowly turned, cocking his head in her direction. "Who do I share it with?"

"Me. And the others in the group."

Now he was suspicious. "What group?"

She held out her hands, fingers spread, placating. "Trust me. You won't want to do all of this alone." She gestured to the vista deck's high ceiling, and presumably meant one of the floors above them in the Med Center. "There are two social organizations—they meet on the sixtieth—for those who have fallen under the Laviola's affliction."

"Hammered." He said the word sharply, but without much force, not much like a hammer.

"Write down everything that occurs to you, every dream that seizes you. Keep a record of life, a map of the places you will experience."

"What about thoughts? I have things in my head that surface and make themselves known, but they're not my thoughts." He unfolded a piece of notepaper, crumpled and tight in one fist, and read the lines he had put down that morning,

"Some saw the tracks like a flower's opening petals in spring. Others saw a spider's web, beautiful in its ability to move with the winds between worlds, and resist the tension and strain of extraordinary weight along the thousand fibers."

She just nodded.

Benecka set Huan up in a support group, returning later to gather feedback, but he didn't want to talk about it—one bland meeting with a bunch of psychos was enough to kill the community feeling he was supposed to have. She urged him to continue attending, and he did so only because he had promised. He went to three more meetings.

He fell back on the only bright substance in his life. He took Wallace's words to heart: Understand the Laviolanis.

You're tagged now. How would Wallace know what it felt like? The question troubled him, but he heard his teacher's words loudly. *Live it. Understand the life of which you've become a part.* It sounded stale, but it was the only bond he had with reality, Wallace's continual exhorting his students to follow him, become like him. That was all Huan had left. That, and the dreams of suffocating darkness that choked off his breath, dropping the temp in his body. Waking up ...

... to a shadowy human shape with a gun standing in the bedroom of his new apartment.

Huan stared at the man and the weapon, not really frightened. "Wait, let me guess, you're going to kill me?"

The man nodded, pleased, as if he was rarely surprised, but

genuinely enjoyed it when someone was able to pull it off. "Well done, Mr. Norr."

"But ..." What do you tell a killer who bluntly agrees with you? And Huan was really awake now.

One side of the killer's mouth curled sourly. "Except someone got here before me, I see." Smile fading, he didn't sound happy about it. The killer shook his head, and holstered his gun under the folds of his dark jacket. He indicated the two bat-like creatures that had taken to Huan like pets, one nestled under his arm, the other perched on the headboard. "How long you been tagged?"

"Fourteen days." It was a mystery for a while, but psychOps pulled it out of his memories, Huan bumping into the blond man in the hall, handing him the weird thorny plant, its stem and sharp defense system coated with the sap from the Laviola at Siddaq. Tagging was one of Azzarito's crueler methods for ending someone's life. More like destroying it through an extended process of torture and pain, the ability to assassinate someone with a long, ugly, drawn out death.

It wasn't that you couldn't live a long life while hammered, but you wouldn't want to. And there was the general view that being hammered was worse than death.

"Poor bastard." Norr's latest killer commented—with some sympathy, then lifted his chin to the open window. "And you moved this close to Siddaq Reach, to the thing that controls you?"

The Laviola's central spire jutted up from the coastline, in view from the window, an inverse pyramid of glowing white foliage bleeding into pale blue, veined in brown and blood-red. The central structure climbed twenty meters into the sky, crowned in vivid green blossoms with ten-meter long petals that curled back to the planet, flapping like pennants in the sea breeze. Four highway-width bands of leafy material stretched out three kilometers from the Laviola's core, a perfect cross, two in line with the planet's axis, the other two perpendicular to it.

"I am ..." his voice failed. He was going to spout some Wallace at him, but ended up with a faint, "I don't have a choice."

No need to waste rounds. Huan was already dead—or worse, driven into death by the madness the Laviolas planted in their victims. Huan heard the sympathy in the killer's voice when he wished him luck—just before hopping through the window and vanishing.

Every day the hammers came for more of him. A couple of them moved in, permanent residents after he stopped fighting them. He had scars running up his legs, more along his shoulders, and he was constantly washing his blood from the bedding.

Damned inconvenient.

The suffocating nightmares continued and could strike at any time. Huan had been studying Wallace's travels all morning, just coming to the realization that he hadn't been hit with a nightmare for hours. He took a few steady breaths, tensing up around the notion that it was just the calm before a storm. And then he collapsed during lunch, shivering, immersed in the same icy fluid that held his body rigid, stilled his breath. Huan's anger raged against the helplessness, and ... it worked. He forced himself into the dream and managed to shift his head to the right, just the simple one-axis movement at first, then almost chin to shoulder and a decent range of motion forward and back. He pulled his hands into claws, but Huan couldn't reach a hard fist.

He woke with Benecka pounding on his door. She brought him a tissue culture kit that allowed him to grow what were basically tumors for the hammers to feed on so they wouldn't take parts of him that he required ... or were really fond of. He had a nice knobby row of them across his stomach when she left. And his two hammers found them satisfactory.

In the hours, and sometimes days, between bouts of madness he searched through the botany journals and books, scanned biographical details, digging through years-old records of his hated teacher.

Follow in his footsteps, Wallace urged him from his lecture notes. What did he want, for him to get offworld? Return to Earth? Seek him out?

Huan might have been Wallace's premier student, but socially he was nobody, no clout, no great wealth. He would be captured at the gates, and sent to spend the rest of his life in some tagged prison ward. Wallace had always been somebody, had extraordinary wealth, had favors that could be called in, had ways of getting offworld. The thought hit him ... like a hammer—the old-fashioned kind.

Wallace is tagged.

Follow in his footsteps! Not return to Earth. Where did he go when he studied here? What paths did he take?

Huan hit the library services, trying to track down more of Wallace's decades-old notes. So much had been purged with the hate that followed Wallace's departure, that Huan had to turn to underground sources, finding knowledge suppliers who didn't like him—or really, didn't like what he stood for—but had access to files and document scans that no one else on the planet had.

In desperation he read his sparse notes on Wallace's Lassandran travel lectures. He had never paid much attention to them, considering them general interest, not science, and often tedious.

Wallace was tagged. He fled Lassandra for the safety of Earth. He had survived by going virtual.

Huan shoved out a breath and went still. He was trying to get his thoughts around another connection that had gnawed at him for days. Wallace had never stopped insisting that the range was unlimited, and that, wherever you ran, the bats would hunt you down and take their meal. Huan shook it off.

Finally he dropped everything he had gathered over the months, and just focused on the first two lines of Wallace's travelogue.

Footsteps, one at a time. Begin at home.

Huan rifled through his notes for what came after the journey's beginning.

He tossed away the botany texts and journals, and put everything he had into learning whole new fields of study, entirely new ways of looking at old studies. Until he reached the boundaries of the old, and had to clear new and unsteady paths— new studies he was calling angiochemistry and holobotany. He had to learn new geometries, new ways of seeing, new languages that presented the structure of connected biological worlds in new ways. Until he went through the irregular holes he was cutting—daily—from the cloth of his original purpose. Until nothing substantial remained of it, and he could not remember why he had agreed—with his whole heart—to Philip Wallace's "extended research" plan. Until moving through the loose threads of what had been his purpose—and coming out the other side— did not frighten him anymore.

And that's where Huan Norr planted the seeds of his new life.

Benecka checked on him every ten days or so. She found him once dancing around his apartment, shouting, "Wallace was right!" while both of his hammers shifted their wings to remain perched on his shoulders. She gave him a sour look, and said he was in "a deep mental dive."

Wallace was right. The Laviolan life cycle couldn't rely solely on tracking the tag scent of its symbionts. There must be some other trail the hammers followed, no distance too great for the Lassandran Chiropterans' ranging methods.

He tested every new idea, traveled in the footsteps of Sir Philip, climbed the Walzier range at nine-thousand meters, and they found him, his little bat-like friends.

He boarded a sub-orb bus at Metee, and spent a week on the other side of the planet at the edge of a seventy-kilometer ellipse of baked sand where it looked like some past interstellar traveler had set down a large ship. It was a tourist attraction on Lassandra, an alien landing strip thing. He milled in the heat with thousands of Lassandrans ... and the hammers found him among them.

After five months, Huan went home to Siddaq to plot the next leg of the journey.

The nightmares continued, smooth cave walls pressing in him, his body steeping in the same cold fluid, movement restricted to a head turn, a toe curl, but never enough strength to draw air into his lungs. A burst of light hit his unused eyes. He choked up freezing liquid. Something from inside the dream pushed him outside.

Huan's eyes shot open.

He sat up, breathing hard, and felt a pull on his thought, a thread knotted deep in cognitive tissue, and a voice he knew almost as well as his own was tugging on it. He felt the presence, at least as strong as the weight of doubt and insanity. He kept his voice low, his own ears fearing to hear it aloud.

"Sir Philip?"

It was all in his head, but he heard or felt him release a long breath. "Huan? It's me. They brought my body out of suspension."

Huan snapped out of the shock, and concentrated on getting his breathing under control. "How?"

"How are we communicating?"

He nodded, and he felt Wallace's response.

"You've bonded, for starts. I'm trying to make 'bonding' the canonical term, instead of tagging, which is pejorative. The Laviola is a hub, and there are bridges linking all of its bondmates. There's a mouth into the network at each node."

He already knew the answer, but *you have to begin with a question.* "You are tagged, correct?"

"Bonded."

"And we never knew?"

"I never told you. Illegal off Lassandra. I mean, it's importing-alien-viral-mechanisms illegal."

Questions bubbled up and Huan had to ask them. "And do the bats come for you ... to feed? Even on Earth?"

"Three of them. I've hidden them all these years. And ..." He paused. "... there's a juvenile Laviolanis growing—as we speak—on the grounds of my manor in Costa Rica."

A stab of shock, and then the facts punched through it like tree roots finding a seam in rock. "The Laviolanis bears no fruit, no seeds. How?"

"I swear I brought nothing back with me."

Huan drew a long breath, turning this over in his thoughts.

Sir Philip went on eagerly, "Two quick things. New direction. Drop your non-phototropic nonsense. The scope's too narrow."

"I already have. I'm finishing up two research pieces, one on a new field I'm calling angiochemistry."

Wallace's voice came back bright in his own head. "Excellent! I knew you were the one to do it. The bridging the Laviola creates is so much deeper than anything botany can teach us. So much more important. Our jumpships follow holes through space that someone else left, rough needle holes, like a tailor's mistake. But they're good enough. They allow us to travel the distance between Earth and Lassandra in a little over a decade instead of centuries. Maybe those holes are mistakes, left behind when the thread was pulled out, and sewn into more direct seams? Just think about that, think about what the Laviolanis species has done, or grown into. Listen to the two of us, to what we're doing right now. We're talking through them. They stretch between star systems, from you to me. Realtime."

After a moment's pause, Huan said, "You said two quick things. What's the second?"

"Oh, yes. Stop trying to contact me."

Huan lurched, hands going up automatically, as if to stifle

the guilt in his voice. "I haven't sent a single message." So much had happened, and he hadn't sent any of his new work—or even a simple status to his own teacher.

"Dreams of dying? Nightmares?" Wallace threw out a few hints.

Huan nodded vigorously. "I have them all the time. As if I can't breathe. Darkness. Cold. Helpless. I've never had nightmares like these."

"You should see the ones you've given the techs here in the suspension lab. You've frightened the wits out of them."

"I don't understand."

"It's why they pulled me out of virtual. My suspended body warmed to critical—on its own! It twitched, moved its head, opened its mouth, jumping around in the fluid as if it was trying to wake up. It was you from Lassandra, pushing yourself into my suspended body, trying to contact me."

Huan felt a bolt of heat run through his body, shock, a flood of understanding that kept him silent.

Wallace could feel it. "I know. I know. We have to close this down until we truly comprehend it. Who knows how far it stretches or who's included in our conversation. It could take in other worlds. Don't you see? The paths may lead to every one of us at once. It leads to me, wherever I go, it stretches through space, pinning me down. And the nightmares, the madness, the symptoms of being tagged—sorry, bonded?" The excitement in Wallace's voice climbed several notches. "It isn't madness at all! We just didn't understand it. I've suffered them for seventy years, taking neuroblockers and short-term dip suspends to escape them. Huan, you broke through! It's clear to me now. It isn't insanity! The dreams happen when one of us falls or we force ourselves into the transmission network. When we expend the effort to generate a link to some other node. Imagine the shock to a living system, on both sides, emerging in someone else's space, losing momentary control over your own body. Horrifying, if you don't understand what's happening. We can see through the eyes of others who've been tagged—bonded. We can fit into their thoughts, move in their forms, become them for pulses of time."

"Living system? Wait, the insanity is ... some of them ... may not be human?"

"Or even alive!" Sir Philip paused. "What exactly does the Laviolanis take when it bonds with us? What has it taken from us, or what have we given it, Huan? Is the Lavi a portal of some kind, machinery, a new phyla, a plant, an animal, what is it? That is what we must discover, my greatest student. You have already started. You already know the path. We must begin again. Not as botanists, but as children, open to any question, willing to weigh every option, take any chance, set our feet down on a new landscape. A new order of existence requires a new beginning, even if we must approach with cautious steps."

Huan nodded slowly, a chill running through him. *How was I chosen to be here, to be the one to break into the channel?* He bowed his head, shaking. A surge of strength from his teacher kept him from losing his footing. "I would give my life to help you find out, Philip."

Huan's own pledge folded into Wallace's response, "We have done that already, you and I."

Chris Howard *is just a creative guy with a pen and a paint brush, author of* Seaborn *(Juno Books, 2008),* Salvage *(Masque/Prime Books, 2013),* Nanowhere *(Lykeion, 2005), and a shelf-full of other books. His short stories and essays have appeared in various zines and anthologies, including "Lost Dogs and Fireplace Archeology" in* Fantasy Magazine *and "How to Build Worlds Without Becoming the Minister for Tourism" in* Now Write! Science Fiction, Fantasy and Horror *(Penguin, 2014). His story "The Mermaid Game" appeared in the Paula Guran edited anthology* Mermaids and Other Mysteries of the Deep *(Prime, 2015), and "Hammers and Snails" was a Robert A. Heinlein Centennial Short Fiction Contest winner. Chris writes and illustrates the comic* Saltwater Witch. *His art has appeared on dozens of book covers, in* Shimmer, BuzzyMag, *various RPGs, and on the pages of books, blogs, and other interesting places. Chris is a Science Fiction & Fantasy Writers of America (SFWA) member. Find out more here: www.SaltwaterWitch.com*

For the Sake

Scott Davis

Golem perches on a coffee shop pedestal. The air around his head moves and whispers. He bores a hole in the wall with his stare until the waitress blocks those twin beams with her torso and says, "What brings you to our fair city?"

"There has been a crime," Golem replies.

A cop on the next stool leans over, too dull to realize he's in another kind of space when he gets that close. "I didn't think there were any laws left to violate. Look." He pulls out a thick wad of large denomination bills and shoves it under Golem's nose. It smells of fresh ink. "We don't want any trouble."

Golem turns.

The cop's bladder reminds him of its bloated discomfort.

Golem says, "Only retribution will restore balance"

"Have it your way." The cop feels for his handcuffs with his left, his pistol with his right, then stops. His skin dries like an apple core left out, his eyes a gasoline stain on water. He becomes various kinds of garbage, falling off the stool and apart on the floor. The waitress screams.

SCOTT DAVIS

A twenty appears under Golem's saucer. Golem dons his felt hat and opens the glass door to the street. *Quickly!*, chirps the bird at Golem's ear. *Now they know.*

"There is no 'they'", Golem reminds the bird. "Each is alone. Just suggest to each that the cop had leprosy, which is true in a way."

Bulbous yellow taxis make more noise than progress hooting around corners in the night. Alleys and parks are miasmas most skirt out of terror.

Golem feels a lifting, incongruous, coming from an alley, and so enters. The overweight grey bird in the rag pile is a snoring angel, sloe gin fifth clutched up. Golem rattles a trash can lid. The angel stirs, then starts at the sight of Golem. Rat tails disappear under rotted doors.

"Remember yourself," Golem says.

The angel tries his sooty wings, but only flails, looking abashed. At length he takes unsteady flight, provoking cat yowls and, as he ascends past a cloudy apartment window, the screams of small caged birds convinced they're about to be devoured by a giant owl. Above the streetlights, his wing beats are soon lost to jackhammer spits and siren wails as the darkness takes him. Golem turns into the path of a knife.

"Your money," a voice drips.

Golem turns his palms out. His pants are pocket-less and his tunic simple. The mugger paces around him, knife like a clock hand facing inward.

"Who do you think you are? Some kind of kung fu guy? Give me that fedora! Doesn't match anyway." He chuckles at his fine fashion sense. "And pull your pants down. No one gets away from

Sammy free."

Sammy's right arm withers a hundred years. He yelps like a beaten dog and catches the falling knife with his left hand just as that arm ages as well. The blade jangles on the asphalt.

"Jennifer needs you. She doesn't have any good veins left. Go home while you can still walk," Golem says to the hunched, whimpering figure then walks out of the alley. A third floor apartment window isn't completely dark. The bird flutters up to it. *A poor man shares his supper,* the bird reports.

Golem's face falls. For the sake of such, the city continues. The Father spoke, the Son nodded, but they don't come down, hell no. Who do they send? The most worthless of the three, puny bird. And me. The weight of that decision turns Golem's thoughts slow and brown, hunches his posture and scuffles his sandals.

Golem looks into a church, ghost children crowding the narthex. They look at him, yearning for release. He looks among them, but doesn't see her.

In a hospital basement, Golem finds her. The ghost of the little girl sits on a metal cart, crying. Her body lies under the sheet behind her—only the feet exposed—toe-tagged. Golem notes the address on the tag. She looks through bleary eyes and says, "I want my Mommy!"

"She sold your heart."

"Why won't I get up?"

"You're alive now, not incarnate."

"I'm scared."

"You don't need that emotion."

"Who are you? How do you know?"

Golem lumbers onto an empty cart and exhales, "He gave

me this job, and as long as there's something salvageable down here, I have to go on.

"Who is He?"

"You know."

"How long have you been doing this?"

"Ever since angels fell down on the job."

The ghost looks someplace else. "Is all that for me?"

"Yes, but they won't get too close. We have to take the first steps."

As they ascend into the brilliance. Golem releases her hand. A glowing white one takes hers with infinite gentleness. She turns. "Aren't you coming too?"

The growing distance makes Golem's reply increasingly faint. "Soon I hope. First, I must pay your mother a visit."

Scott Davis has a small business to do with legal help for prisoners. He has a baker's dozen of writing credits. He mourns Ray Bradbury's death, but as long as there is a Bradbury story he hasn't read, The Master lives.

Frozen Moments

Talib S. Hussain

Mirror

"Now where did my hairbrush go?" Lina called as she entered the master bathroom. "It was right here a few minutes ago."

Tom quietly laughed as he whispered "leave no trace." He waited a few moments before responding. "Maybe you left it in the kids' room?"

As Lina dashed off to find the brush, Tom glanced at his reflection in the bedroom mirror and gave himself a self-satisfied smile.

A few minutes later, Lina re-entered the bedroom, took one look at Tom standing there in his underwear and exclaimed, "Get ready! You're making us late ... as usual."

"Yeah, yeah, there's no rush," Tom replied, "It's just a party."

Lina shook her head and left the room. "I'm getting the kids ready to go in the car—hurry up."

Tom quickly finished getting dressed. Before leaving the bedroom, he picked up his watch from the nightstand and wound it up before putting it on. It was a gift his dad had given to him many years ago, and he never went anywhere without it. A lovely manual watch with a subsecond hand in addition to the normal second, minute and hour hands, and a clear back that let you see the mechanisms in action.

Good Things

Half an hour later, the family was finally all ready to go. Both kids were in the station wagon in their car seats in the back. Sophia, their two-and-a-half-year-old daughter was on the passenger side and Kevin, their six-month-old son was behind Tom on the driver's side. The diaper bag was in the car, and the kids each had a bottle and a toy.

It was a warm evening and Lina was aggressively rolling down the window as Tom got in his seat. "Why do you always insist on buying the lowest model cars, Tom?" she huffed, repeating one of her famous complaints. Tom replied with his usual, "Well, they were good enough for my dad, so they're good enough for me."

Lina shook her head in fake exasperation and switched mental gears. "Wallets, purse, cell phones, gift—where's the gift?" Lina asked.

"Last I saw, it was on the shelf next to the attic door where you put it," Tom replied.

"Ah right ... can you please go get it, honey? Oh, and make sure the stove is off."

Tom sighed as he got out of the car and went back in the

house. "The stove was okay," he said as he returned a few moments later to the car and handed the wrapped gift to his wife.

"Wow, that was fast, did you run up the stairs or something?"

Tom smiled and gave them his patented response — "Clark Kent." He mimed taking off his glasses, "Superman!"

"Super, super, super!" Sophia chanted as Lina shook her head at her silly husband.

"Okay. We're off!" Tom said as he put the gear shift into reverse and backed the car out of the driveway.

"We off!" yelled Sophia. "Off off off off off!" she continued gleefully.

Tom and Lina exchanged their "She's soooo cute" look.

Sun is Going Down

"So, who's going to be there, again?" Tom asked as they merged onto the highway.

"My mom invited a few of her friends from work. Other than that, it should be the usual—my sister and brother, Uncle James, and her neighbors," Lina replied.

"Cool. What's for dinner? Any idea?"

Lina smiled, knowing that Tom's priorities in life were sleep and food (after, of course, his wife and children). "Just you wait and see—you're so impatient," she chided.

"Daddy, daddy," cried Sophia. "Pretty colors."

Tom glanced back at Sophia, who was pointing out the window at the sky.

"Yes, it's a very pretty sunset," Tom said.

"Pretty pretty pretty pretty," Sophia chanted.

Lina joined in, "Pretty pretty pretty."

Big Truck

As they approached their exit, little Kevin decided to make his presence known. "AAAAAAAA," he cried.

"What's wrong with him?" Tom asked.

"He dropped his toy," Lina said, as she twisted and reached to the rear floor. "Hold on Kevin, Mama will get your toy."

A long noisy minute later, "AAAAAAAAAAAHH ... mmm mm mmm."

"Well, mission save-the-toy accomplished!" Tom said. "Good job."

As they came off the exit ramp to a stop sign, Sophia shouted "Truck! BIG Truck."

An 18-wheeler passed through the intersection in front of them. "Yes, that's a big big truck Sophia," Lina said.

"That's a big big big big BIG one," Sophia declared.

"Big big big one," Tom and Lina echoed, laughing, as they turned left onto the main street.

Slide

A mile later, a flashing arrow indicated a reduction down to one lane.

"Looks like they are re-doing the road," Lina said.

"I hope so. The potholes here are crazy," Tom said.

They quickly caught up to the truck that had passed them and Tom settled in a few cars lengths behind it. "I wonder if there will be scalloped potatoes," Tom mused aloud, "I love your mom's scalloped potatoes."

As the truck in front of them went through the next intersection, Sophia cried happily "That's a big BIG truck."

"It sure is," Tom laughed.

Suddenly, Lina screamed, and as Tom turned his head towards her, he saw a second tractor-trailer bearing down on their passenger side from the cross-street. He slammed the clutch and brakes, and the car started to slide out of control as the brakes locked.

Tom blinked.

Stretch the Frozen Moments

It was suddenly much darker, as usual, but the tableau in front of him was clear.

The oncoming truck was about three feet from the passenger side of the station wagon, its single working headlight glowing an eerie red. Lina was looking out the window and her mouth was open wide in shock. Sophia had her hands pressed against her ears and was staring out the window at the truck with big eyes. The speedometer of the car indicated twenty-seven miles per hour.

It was deadly quiet. Nothing moved, at least not visibly, except for Tom.

Tom's heart beat strongly as he tried to calm himself. He was grateful as never before for the gift that his father's genes had given him. Releasing the brakes and leaving the car in neutral (manual always manual), he unlocked his door (always manual) and opened it. Stepping out on the road, he surveyed the scene. The sun, deep red in color, hung low in the sky in front of the car.

The truck that they had been following was a good forty feet away. There were no other vehicles in sight. The road in front of the car was slightly downhill.

"Perfect," he muttered to himself.

He glanced at his watch—the subsecond hand read fifteen out of sixty.

See their Faces

He peeked in the back window at Kevin, who was lying back in his car seat with his eyes closed and his toy loosely held in his hand.

"Good boy, stay asleep," Tom said, knowing that Kevin couldn't hear him, but needing to say it anyways.

Tom pulled a magazine from the pouch on the back of the driver's seat and placed it on the ground behind the rear driver's-side tire. He then leaned into the car frame on the driver's-side doorway and started to push. Slowly, slowly, the car started to move forward.

After about ten subjective minutes of pushing, Tom stopped to take a break. He glanced back—the tire was about three inches from the magazine. The truck hadn't moved any appreciable distance.

"Better than I had hoped," he said after doing some math in his head, taking into account the real velocities of the car and truck, plus what he could add by pushing. "But, damn Dad! It's going to be too damned close." These days, he often found himself talking aloud to his recently-departed father, who had frequently warned him of the importance of keeping his power secret—even from loved ones. "Always leave no trace" had been his dad's mantra, and Tom had dutifully kept quiet and careful over the years.

No Recourse

"Better safe than sorry, Dad. I'll figure out a way to explain it all, somehow." Making his mind up, Tom opened the back door and disconnected Kevin's infant seat from its base. He carried the seat a good thirty yards down the road behind them and set it down in the grass off the closed lane behind the traffic cones.

Back to the car he went. The truck was too close to open the passenger doors wide enough, so he crawled in the back seat from the driver's side. He unlatched the belt and latch securing Sophia's car seat. Gently, slowly, ever so slowly he dragged Sophia's seat to the driver's side of the car, taking take to support her legs. He lifted the entire seat out of the car, slowly, and carried it over next to Kevin. He paused a moment to look at his quiet, still children. "I love you both" he said, and kissed each of them on the top of their head.

Back to the car again for Lina. Reaching across the center console, he undid her seat belt and carefully threaded it under her arm to remove it. "Pole, pole, Honey," he said softly as he began to move her limbs—something they said often to each other ever since their Swahili-speaking guides had taught them the key to success on their honeymoon hiking trip up Mt Kilimanjaro together ("polay, polay"—slowly, slowly). Of course, it took on a deeper, more dangerous meaning for him now.

Keep the Anger In

Several tries later—"Fuck, fuck, fuck, fuck, FUUUCK!" Tom shouted. He simply couldn't lift Lina safely across the center of the car, and he knew that dragging her across might cause her irreparable harm in this state. He gave her cheek a soft kiss, and went back to pushing the car.

Two Suns

Three hours of subjective time later, Tom had succeeded in pushing the station wagon about four and a half feet ahead. He was exhausted and needed to take longer and longer breaks between bouts of pushing. He glanced at his watch—the subsecond hand now read seventeen. Ironically, it felt to him like time was rushing past. He looked carefully at the relative positions of the car and truck. The front of the truck was now eighteen inches from the car and the car still had another four feet to go before it would definitely clear the truck's path. He could now open the front passenger door, but it was a tight squeeze to get in past the truck engine—too tight to get Lina out.

After another two hours of pushing, the car had moved another three feet and the truck was now about six inches from the rear end of the car, its headlight shining into Tom's eyes like a huge, evil red eye; like a malevolent sun that strangely matched the setting sun in the sky ahead. Tom's arms and legs were shaking continuously from the extreme exertion.

Race is Run

There was now enough clearance, thankfully. Tom opened the passenger door again and started the hard job of shifting

Lina's body around—ever mindful that moving any joint too fast or in the wrong direction could rupture it. After forty minutes of careful adjustments, he was able to position her over his shoulder in a fireman's carry.

"Woman, you have got to lose some weight!" he grunted as he lifted her up and edged her carefully around the door and away from the truck engine, now only a couple inches from impacting the car bumper. His back burned with pain—he was certainly past his limit.

Tom walked diagonally away from the truck and car. After fifteen yards, his back began to go completely. He lowered himself to his knees and slowly leaned sideways until Lina was lying on the ground.

"I hope that's enough", he said as he collapsed, his back seizing.

Hear their Voices

4/60ths of a second had passed since the start of this adventure. Tom watched, prone on the ground as the trunk inched closer and closer. From his vantage point, it looked like it could go either way. To keep his options open in case of an accident, he simply let time creep by for as long as he could. Many subjective minutes later, he jolted awake when Lina and the kids screamed and the truck blared its horn as it continued down the road, unscathed.

Confirmed Suspicions

The drive to dinner seemed to take forever. They probably should have canceled and gone home, but Lina had insisted on going in a bid for normalcy. "We're going, and that's that, you liar," Lina had exclaimed after his initial explanations in the aftermath of the near accident. She really hadn't wanted to hear the details once she realized that he had been holding out on her, and had settled into a stormy, stressed silence as she drove the car the few remaining miles.

"Are we okay, honey?" Tom asked Lina, as they arrived at her mom's house. Lina's response, a glare and a slammed door, was about what he expected. Tom woke the kids, who had fallen asleep from the stress, and braced himself for a difficult evening.

Dinner, while tasty, was quite strained, with Lina sitting on the far end of the table and alternating between glaring at him and being on the verge of tears. The family had left it alone, but knew something was up. It didn't help that he kept nodding off, only to wake up trembling at the thought of how close everything had been.

Equal in the End

Finally, just as the main course was wrapping up, Lina walked over and whispered in his ear. "It was you. The hairbrush. You moved my hairbrush—didn't you?" There was a hint of wonder in her accusation.

"I admit nothing," said Tom—their pet code for yes—as he lifted, gingerly because of his back, his last forkful of scalloped potatoes to his mouth. Everything would work out, he had faith—but it would certainly be interesting for a while.

"That's a big big big BIG bite, Daddy!"

Glancing at his watch and thinking of his own father, Tom replied, once he had swallowed, "Yes, it certainly is a very big bite."

Talib S. Hussain *enjoys writing poems and short stories in the cracks between his researcher day job and his many activities as husband and father (of two wonderful children who may or may not have borne a resemblance to certain characters in this story not so long ago). His poem "Super Sense" appeared in* Flying Higher: An Anthology of Superhero Poetry *edited by Shira Lipkin and Michael Damian Thomas. He has written many scientific publications, including, as co-editor, the book* Design and Development of Training Games: Practical Guidelines from a Multi-disciplinary Perspective *published by Cambridge University Press. He has also written an unpublished children's story,* Purple Worms, *which met with rave reviews in public readings at both of his children's kindergarten classes – which is all the reward he needed. You can find out more about his current creative pursuits at talibhussain.net.*

Road To Redemption

LJ Cohen

Jayce thumbed through the sheaf of well worn bills, keeping Reverend Larkin in her peripheral vision. He didn't look like the picture on the back of his books or on his website, but sleeping in the same clothes for a night or two can do that to you.

"It's all there," he said. As haggard as he looked, his voice was still better suited to the stage or the camera than to the front seat of her pick-up. Easy to see how he persuaded the faithful to empty their pockets into his personal ministry. He was fully Human, though, despite the seductive voice.

She frowned, staring out the windshield at the rain-damp street. He made it sound like a routine job. Transport one man from point A to point B. All the money up front. But he was entirely too confident for her typical client. What what he doing here? People like him had limousines and entourages, not one Sensitive in a tired truck.

Larkin's money had passed through too many hands. Jayce wanted to wash hers, though that never prevented the emotional assault. She slipped the bills back in the envelope.

So many desperate people. As tough as things were around town, Larkin's revival meetings had been standing room only. Hard times always seemed to swell church coffers. Something she and Larkin had in common—both their jobs were recession-proof.

"I'm sure it is, Mr. Larkin." She emphasized the "Mr" and pretended not to notice his frown.

"That is your fee, Miss Techler, isn't it?"

He stressed the "Miss". For the hundredth time since his message brought her here, she wondered how the hell he'd found out about her. She deliberately put the envelope down on the console between them. He kept his gaze on her face, not the money.

"Sorry. I can't help you."

Larkin examined his clean and buffed fingernails. "We're both business people, Miss Techler. How much for your services?"

"Take your money back," she said, sliding the envelope toward him. "I'm not interested."

That surprised him and Jayce got the sense little surprised Larkin. In her world, his sort of smug complacency got you dead.

He's scared, Jayce. He had to come to you. I bet he's never asked for help before.

She hated it when Topper's voice argued with her. It wasn't fair. His ghost hadn't hung around long enough to say goodbye, so her own memories were doing a good job haunting her in his place.

Larkin met her eyes with his intense blue gaze. If he wore contact lenses, they were very, very good ones. Even on the run, in rumpled clothes he was charismatic. She could resent him for that alone.

He nodded and tucked the money back in his jacket. "I

forgive you and God bless you."

Jayce snorted. "Save it for someone who needs to buy their way into salvation." There was nothing waiting for her at the end of the line. Not even Topper.

"Then I thank you for your time, Miss Techler."

More polite than she deserved. Jayce squelched a pang of guilt as Larkin placed his hand on the door latch. A tremor danced across her skin. Another followed. Her nerve endings lit up like the sky on the fourth of July. Suckers. Tracking Larkin. They were close. Too close. "Shit."

She slammed the stick into drive and floored it. The engine growled as the truck lurched forward, tires scrabbling for purchase.

His composure was as otherworldly as the forces after him. He didn't even ask a single question as she took what must have seemed like crazy, random turns through the mostly abandoned downtown. It didn't matter. Jayce knew where she was. Topper used to tease her she was part homing pigeon.

"Not now," she muttered. Larkin shot her a look, but she just gritted her teeth and kept driving. The back of her neck prickled with warnings. Her instincts took over.

Their pursuers were still too close.

Larkin hadn't told her it was Suckers. If the Suckers found them, it wouldn't only be Larkin who got drained.

The thrumming slowly faded and then it was gone. Jayce took a deep breath and pulled into the empty parking lot of an abandoned big box store, her hands shaking on the steering wheel. Her pulse pounded in her ears.

Larkin pulled out the thick envelope and leaned over to tuck it behind her window visor. "Thank you."

"You son of a bitch." She put the truck into park but left the key in the ignition. "I should just let them have you." Even she wasn't that much of a monster. No matter that the good Reverend believed people like her were damned. "Do you have any idea what they do to Sensitives?" He shook his head. Of course he didn't. "I should charge you double."

"If you can get me safely out of here, I'll see to it that my Church rewards you."

"What will they do, pray over me?" Her mother had tried and it hadn't helped. She doubted Larkin's flock would have any more luck.

"Is that such a terrible thing?"

She wanted to wipe the sincerity off his face. With her fists. "If you do everything I tell you and we're very, very lucky, we might just live through the day."

"I am not afraid of death."

Jayce laughed. Then why was he in her truck? "You're a bad liar Reverend Larkin."

He smiled at her and it erased days of worry and fatigue from his face. The man was charming. But she had known that. No one got to be where he was without the ability to manipulate and dazzle. "I didn't say I wanted to meet my maker today," he said, his too-blue eyes twinkling with unexpected humor. "But my soul is pure and my heart light."

Jayce shook her head. She figured he was just a snake oil salesman, selling a particularly caustic flavor of snake oil. But now it looked like he was drinking the stuff, too. As long as he didn't expect her to take a sip.

"We have a long day ahead. The rain will slow us down on the road. Not them. How badly do they want you?"

"Does it matter?"

Jayce wanted to scream, but she just gripped the steering wheel harder. "Answer the question."

He sat up taller and fixed her in his gaze. "The Lord called upon me to baptize the demons. In His name."

"You what?" Her instincts screamed it was time to run. Just leave him the truck and her gear and get the hell out. "Do you have any idea what you've done?"

"Yes. The Lord's work. I don't expect you to understand."

How could he be so damned calm? "Demons." Jayce shook her head again. Well, if any of the Old Bloods were demons, the Suckers fit the profile. "I should break both your legs and leave you for them as a peace offering."

"I don't believe you would do that."

"After you just singlehandedly demolished the treaties?" It had only been six years since the last of the Blood Wars ended. Not that anyone would call the current situation peace. Not with the Suckers at the top of the heap.

He kept his gaze on her face. "Even so," Larkin said.

"And what makes me so trustworthy? I've heard your gospel of purity."

"The Lord led me to you. He wishes you to be redeemed."

"Get out of my truck. Now."

He turned in his seat to face her directly, remorse in his expression. "I think it's too late for that, child."

Revulsion rippled through her. "Don't ever call me that again. Just get out."

"They marked me." He unbuttoned the top three buttons of his wrinkled shirt. Two puncture wounds puckered the flesh just above his collarbone. "Already, my blood and sweat run with abomination."

Jayce closed her eyes and pounded her hands against the steering wheel. "Why aren't you dead yet?"

"My faith is my rock. My Lord my redeemer."

"And Sucker poison is busy tenderizing all your cells. Idiot, you're a walking, talking oven stuffer roast." Why hadn't she sensed it? The Suckers tracking them had. They were following the scent coded in the injected saliva. She had to get rid of him before they found her, too.

"The Lord will purify me."

Jayce laughed, but the coffee curdled in her stomach. "Before or after the Suckers finish you off?"

He smiled and the hands that buttoned up his shirt were rock steady. It was more than she could have managed.

"The Lord will purify my soul, with a little help from my flock. That's why I need you, Miss Techler." He handed her a business card. "You must get me here within the next ..." He glanced down at his wristwatch. It was one of the expensive ones. And probably the real deal. "... ten hours."

CleanSweep Labs. There was a logo of a broom, an address, but no phone number. Redemption, Oregon. Well, that was fitting. "How about the nearest hospital?" If they caught it early enough, a total transfusion and a bone marrow transplant might give him a fighting chance. It was experimental and expensive, but Jayce figured the church would pony up. Larkin was their public face. The sooner she could deliver him somewhere safe, the sooner she could decontaminate her truck.

Larkin shook his head. "My mission is there."

Mission. He was also a lunatic. A lunatic trying to ignite a new Holy War. Baptizing Suckers. The symbols of the Reverend's faith would infuriate them. And a rational Sucker was bad enough.

Money or no money, Larkin gave her little choice. As long as he was in her care, in her truck, she shared his risk. But the Reverend was right about one thing: she wouldn't abandon anyone to the Suckers. Not even the fanatic who had killed Topper. He had believed he was doing God's work, too.

Jayce tore out of the empty parking lot, her truck's wheels kicking up gravel in a rooster tail. She was a damned Sensitive, not some ninja. Mostly what she did was keep folks who were on the run under the radar until they got someplace safe. Humans, Old Bloods, or Mixed Bloods. What happened after that wasn't her concern. It made use of her talents and she guessed she represented something like neutral ground. And until now, she'd managed to keep clear of the Suckers. Of all the Old Bloods, they never looked for her services, and she never looked for them. It was an arrangement that kept her alive so far.

"Get some sleep," Jayce said, keeping her eyes on the road. "Best case scenario, we've got few hours of driving ahead of us."

"You are not what I expected."

She snorted. As if most Humans could tell that there were monsters in their midst. That was her job. Her mother never told her who or what her father was, but his Old Blood ran through her veins. And for whatever reason, it tangled with her mother's genetic pattern to make Jayce a Sensitive.

Larkin closed his eyes and Jayce exhaled slowly. She would ensure his safe passage, but she didn't have to talk to him.

"Thank you for letting me sleep."

She shrugged. The quiet had been a blessing. Even Topper's voice hadn't intruded on the silence.

"Where are we?"

"About forty miles away." They had made decent time.

Larkin looked out the window. "The Interstate would be faster."

"Shut up and let me do my job." She was sticking to secondary roads for as long as she could. "If the Suckers decide to consider your little stunt an act of war, they can compel the Human authorities to help them. The Interstates have traffic cameras."

She saw him nod in her peripheral vision.

He fell silent and Jayce forced her shoulders to relax. The wipers swept the light rain from the windshield with a comforting rhythm. So far, so good. The sooner she could deliver him to the lab, the better. There were only a few cars on the road and none that seemed to be trailing them. She glanced at her speedometer and eased her foot off the accelerator. Getting picked up for speeding would be just plain stupid.

"Were you baptized, Miss Techler?"

"Give it a rest, Reverend. There's no TV camera here." The man was famous for mass blessings and baptisms where the would-be faithful could buy their soul insurance.

"You probably won't believe me, but I preferred the little church I headed in Peterboro."

She struggled to keep her voice even. "Reverend Larkin, I really don't care if you like to dress up in a clown suit and preach to circus elephants." God, that was something Topper might have said. He could always make her laugh, especially when she was angry. She gripped the steering wheel tight enough to turn both sets of knuckles white. "Why would you give a rat's ass what I think? I'm a Mixed Blood. One of the damned who have broken souls. That's why God has cursed us, right?"

"God loves us all, Miss Techler," he said. His voice was soft and full of pity.

It was the last thing Jayce wanted.

"You don't believe that?"

It might have been true, but not for her. Not if you were a monster or a freak. According to Larkin's beliefs, the Old Bloods had no souls, so at least in his theology, she was better off. She was only broken and broken could be fixed, right?

"Leave me the hell alone." Her voice was shrill in the confines of the truck. "I don't believe in God and your church has just started a war that could bury us all."

"Is there nothing you have faith in?" Larkin spoke with the same smooth resonance as he did in his broadcasts.

She let the miles slide by, chewing on his question. "You wouldn't understand." Topper had believed in her, and for a short while with him, she had even believed in herself. But he had been killed for his belief, shot by a man whose faith said Topper was better off dead than loving a Mixed blood.

Flashing lights ahead caught her eye. Shit. There was something she believed in. No situation was so bad it couldn't get worse.

Jayce eased off the accelerator, glancing for a side road. Going through local towns was risky, but stopping for a road block would be worse. One sniff and any Sucker for miles around would flock to them like buzzards to road kill. At least no one knew where they were headed. There were just too many small roads to cover them all. And as long as she kept moving north they should be okay.

The turn signal sounded like a clock's ticking.

"Where are you going?" he asked.

"You either trust me or you don't, Larkin." She wasn't going to explain herself. Not to him.

"I trust in the Lord and He brought me to you."

She rolled her eyes. "Did the Lord tell you how stupid it was to piss off the Suckers?"

He shrugged and winced as the fabric of his shirt rubbed up against the wound beneath. It must hurt like hell, but he didn't complain. She shook her head. Maybe his god did protect fools. "I can't believe you got out of there alive." It was hard not to admire Larkin, at least a little bit. "There aren't too many people I know who would go against the Suckers alone."

"I wasn't alone."

The placid expression on his face didn't change, but Jayce felt a shudder ripple through her. "You left someone behind?" If she hadn't been worried about being trailed, she would have slammed on the truck's breaks and turned around.

"They are martyrs now. God has rewarded their faith," he said, in his even, implacable voice.

She stopped the truck then, not caring who might be watching. "You walked into a nest of Suckers. Okay. It's crazy, but it's your funeral." She swallowed hard, past the lump in her throat. "But you got a bunch of people killed. That's murder. And the last time I read the Ten Commandments, murder was right up there, near the top." Marked or not, she wanted him out of her truck and out of her life. She'd deal with the Suckers later. Somehow. "Take your blood money. The lab is less than ten miles from here. Even if you have to walk, you should get there before the last of your hours is up."

Larkin nodded, ignoring the envelope. "Never doubt that the Lord has plans for you, Jayce Techler." He reached his hand out and she met it with hers, automatically. As their hands clasped together, a jolt of wrongness jumped from his palm to hers. She jerked her hand away as if she had burned herself.

"I can taste it on you." She shuddered. A metallic tang grated against her nerves.

"Did you not realize, Miss Techler?"

She shook her head.

"There was a reason they let me get out of there alive".

The blood drained from her face. "They tried to turn you."

"Yes."

The great Reverend Larkin, transformed not into food, but into one of them. They let him leave, knowing he would turn and come back to them of his own accord. Jayce shivered.

"The treaty you believe I have broken has never been honored by the Suckers."

Deep down, Jayce knew that. She knew also the Blood Wars had been as much a power struggle amongst the factions of Old Bloods as between them and the Humans. In the end, the Old Bloods understood the odds were on the Human's side in sheer population alone and there had been somewhat of a truce since.

The Shifters spent too much time fighting one another for dominance to be a major threat, and the Sidhe wanted nothing more than their beautiful isolation. The Suckers had always been the apex predators, their small numbers effectively culling the Humans. It made them the biggest danger. "I don't understand. Why are you doing this?"

He paused for a long moment before speaking softly. "Have you never risked everything for something you loved?"

Once upon a time, she would have given anything for Topper. And in the end, he had given his life for hers.

He's not such a bad sort, Jayce. Even if he is a religious nut job.

Topper loved channel flipping and watching the televangelists. Even when they had denounced mixed relationships. Their relationship.

"There are members of my flock that have been taken by the Suckers. Tortured. Killed as food. Their souls have been stolen from the hand of God and I have been given this task to redeem them. If I don't get to the lab, it will have been for nothing." Larkin met her gaze with his and she was the one to blink and look away. "What will you do now?"

Jayce buried her head in her hands and laughed until she choked. She couldn't help it. No matter what path she chose, the universe was mocking her. Leave the Reverend by the side of the road and in a matter of hours, he would no longer be Human. And she'd be the first one he'd come after.

She had to get him to his destination. If he survived, he'd start a crusade. It wouldn't be only against the Suckers, but it would spread to any who carried the Old Blood. Including her.

"Even if your fancy lab can reverse the virus, the Suckers will never stop hunting you." She figured the place had some kind of private cure, available for the well-connected. Larkin would definitely count as connected: several presidents had had Larkin speak at their inaugurals.

"Is that what you think?"

"Reverend Larkin, it's what I know." She was too weary to

snap at him. "Even the rest of the Old Bloods are wary of their Sucker brethren. Suckers are pure predators. And we are all just different levels of prey. They will come after you."

"No, child."

Jayce was too exhausted to snap at him for the paternalistic tone of his voice. "You're an idiot," she said softly.

He's scared, Jayce, cut him a little slack.

Topper was always giving people the benefit of the doubt. It's also what got him shot.

"Miss. Techler, whatever you believe, I'm not doing this for myself. The lab has no cure, but someday, with the grace of God and from the virus incubating in my blood, they may be able to develop one. All I ask is that you deliver me to CleanSweep."

Her breath caught in her throat. "You wanted this? You deliberately antagonized the Suckers and used yourself as bait so they would infect you?" She closed her eyes and shook her head. "Jesus!"

When he didn't react to her swearing, she turned to him. His head was downcast and his eyes were closed. At first, she thought he might be praying. As if that would do him any good now, with Sucker poison fighting for control. Sweat beaded his forehead and his cheeks were flushed. Jayce didn't need to touch him to know he was burning up.

"There isn't much time," Larkin said. "Now that the fever has set in, the next stage is convulsions followed by a brief coma. After that, it will be too late." His voice was steady. He could have been commenting on the weather.

Jayce wanted to scream at him, to roll him out of the truck, and keep on driving. "What if we don't make it in time?"

"Then my sacrifice will have been in vain." He opened his

eyes, reached into his jacket pocket, and withdrew a small padded envelope. "Here."

Frowning, she unsealed it and pulled out a plain leather knife pouch. She slid the slim silver blade partway free. It was not much larger than a letter opener, but much, much sharper. Her hands shook and the envelope rustled, too loud in the confined space. "What do you think I am?"

He studied her for a few minutes before answering. "God's hand." His eyes slid shut again.

Jayce put it back in the envelope and set it down in the cup holder with shaking hands. Her best weapons were movement and caution. She was a damned Sensitive. He had to know how much using that knife would hurt her.

A reflection in the rearview mirror caught her eye. A smear of color against the rain. Larkin stiffened, looking to Jayce and the knife. A car approached where they were parked. It slowed as it came even with them, stopping in front of the truck, blocking them in. Larkin hadn't moved, but he was whispering the Lord's Prayer. Her mother had made her memorize it as a child. Before she realized her own daughter was a freak and threw her out.

A tall man walked toward them, his yellow slicker so bright it hurt her eyes. Even before she saw the holster, she'd already pegged him as a cop. He had the measured walk and the confident swagger. Jayce rolled down the window, her body tensing. If he was a Sucker, she couldn't tell. There was already too much of it pouring off Larkin.

"You folks need any help?"

Her hand strayed toward the knife and she jerked it back to the steering wheel. What was she going to do? Stab some local cop? She might as well just turn damned thing on herself and take the damage directly. "Just taking a breather. It's been a long trip."

He nodded, dark hair plastered to his head by the rain. "It's not real safe to stop on the side of the road, ma'am."

Jayce smiled. Suckers would never call their food "ma'am"

"There's a place up the road in Redemption with pretty good coffee. The pie's not bad either."

"Thanks," Jayce said. She took a deep breath. A strong musky maleness poured off him. It was more than a scent she took in with her ordinary senses. The wolf in him was eager, but well controlled. "You live around here?"

"All my life." He smiled and there was no hidden tension in the set of his lips or in his shoulders. Just a local sheriff, stopping to help someone on the road. Who also happened to be a werewolf.

All the Shifters she'd encountered in her messed-up world were desperate, hunted things; outcasts in their families and without pack. He was a lucky bastard.

"If you stop at the coffee shop, tell 'em Officer Milo sent you."

Jayce watched the young Shifter as he walked back to his car with the odd, animal grace they all shared. His car eased back onto the road and drove away. She wondered what his Human mother had thought the first time he changed. Maybe things were different here. The pang of jealousy didn't surprise her. It was an old, familiar pain.

"Still think our souls are broken, Reverend Larkin?"

His lips had stilled. His eyes were moving back and forth in a jagged rhythm through closed lids. Tremors moved through his body, jerking his limbs.

Not broken. Never broken. Topper's voice whispered through memories she had struggled for so long to suppress.

She could sit here and argue with the barely conscious man until he turned or died in the process and it wouldn't bring Topper back. The pain of loss lodged in her chest like the bullet that killed him. But it wasn't Larkin's fault.

And it wasn't hers, either.

Tears streamed down her face like the raindrops on the windshield as she started up the truck again.

LJ Cohen is a poet and novelist, blogger, local food enthusiast, Doctor Who fan, and relentless optimist. After 25 years as a physical therapist, LJ now uses her clinical skills to injure characters in SF&F novels. They include YA fantasy titles, The Between *and* Time and Tithe *in the Changeling's Choice series, and* Future Tense *as well as the first three novels of her SF series, Halcyone Space,* Derelict *(a Library Journal Self-e select title),* Ithaka Rising, *and* Dreadnought and Shuttle. *She lives outside of Boston. LJ is a member of SFWA (Science Fiction and Fantasy Writers of America) and Broad Universe, a national organization promoting women writers of science fiction, fantasy, and horror. You can connect with LJ via her blog: www.ljcbluemuse.blogspot.com and her website: www.ljcohen.net*

The Harvest

KJ Kabza

We should only take what they tell us—or so pompous Faheem declared. "Ice harvesting's a tricky business," he lectured, in my very awkward one-on-one orientation. "You've got to consider the orbits of all the bodies in Diaphana's rings before you act. Remove the wrong icebody, perturb the wrong sets of neighboring orbits and... well."

Well? I figured that Faheem was full of shit. He just likes bossing people—I know the type. And I don't take crap from nobody, so I say, "Next shift, let's just grab the closest icebody and knock off early." My work crew agrees. Nobody else likes Faheem, either.

The nearest icebody to Station XI is only two minutes away. We tow it back, triumphant.

I buy a round of drinks for everyone in the lounge. Faheem can take his rules and shove 'em. We're all laughing and drinking when the empty bottles start to shake. Some fall over. It feels like we're aboard a shuttle on re-entry.

I look out the windows.

Oh, shit.

*For **KJ Kabza**'s bio, see* Sputnik 2, Interior, *p. 2.*

Part II:
Confusion and Change

A Photograph of Silver Moonlight on Black Water

William Gerke

I was tending bar at Farraday's the first time I saw a goddess in the flesh.

It was slow for a Thursday, still early, and the crowd was mostly Boston University students spending their parents' money. A girl leaned over the bar, demanding a Long Island Iced Tea. She couldn't have been more than sixteen, all peaches and cream and bare midriff.

I looked at the door to see if the bouncer was missing or maybe lost his mind letting a teenager in, and that's when I saw Artemis.

From across the room, she hit me like a wave of cold night air and silver moonlight on black water. I couldn't breathe, and I didn't care. Her skin was flawless and olive, and a cascade of dark hair drowned her shoulders. She wore black leather pants and an electric blue silk tunic with a plunging neckline. Silver bangles hung from her wrists, and a silver torc wrapped around her left arm.

Someone snapped their fingers in front of my face. The sound dragged me back to the bar. Peaches-and-Cream gestured towards her friend, an Asian girl in a strappy top.

"Mia wants one, too. And there'll be more coming."

I looked at Kim, who was managing that night. They were underage, but they'd come in with Artemis. She shrugged. What choice did we have? We'd be breaking the law, but the alternative was arguing with a goddess, and we'd both seen the news footage from the incident in Los Angeles.

What followed was an endless parade of froofy drinks with fruit and juices and blenders. The DJ played music to match— dance and pop with a dose of Olympus House, including respectfully-remixed Apollo blocks.

The dance floor seethed with crop tops, capris, mini-skirts, spaghetti straps, high heels, and little black dresses. Ranging from teens to twenties, the slender, firm young bodies twisted in the lights, rubbing against each other and doing everything possible to drive the college boys mad. The smart or strong ones scuttled out as quickly as possible; the rest clung to their seats or were dragged onto the dance floor by nubile girls who ground against them and each other, always flirting, always teasing, always in utter control. You could look but not touch—unless they invited you—and even then touching wouldn't go too far. They were followers of a virgin goddess, after all.

I kept my mind on the job, moving quickly from one drink to the next, head down, keeping a wall of booze between me and the dancers.

One guy tried to step onto the dance floor uninvited, and a brief tussle ensued as his friends dragged him back to their table. I moved to help, but Kim waved me off.

"Stay behind the bar," she said. "It's safer." She pushed her way through the throng. With the help of a waitress, she shuffled the guy to the door, and the bouncer ejected him. I caught one last glimpse of his pale, glassy-eyed face before the door closed.

When she got back, Kim looked me over. Waitress-turned-bartender-turned-manager, she was one of those women who got thin with age, her arms bony but leanly muscled in her sleeveless top, kinky dishwater-blonde hair pulled back tight, skin weathered by years of smoky rooms back before smoking in bars was illegal.

"How're you doing, Ben?" she asked. "You look a little rough."

I nodded. My breathing was shallow, and my shirt clung to my skin. The bar was hot under normal circumstances but packed with nubile virgin girls—well, I'm only human.

"You could go home," said Kim.

I slid two more drinks to a pair of tall, slender women in dresses that hugged athletic bodies. Probably college volleyball or basketball players. Artemis was especially popular with female athletes who claimed abstinence helped them focus.

I took three more orders, speaking to Kim as I passed.

"You need me. There's barely enough of us to handle this."

"I need you tomorrow night, too. I just want to make sure you don't do anything stupid."

"I face temptation every night. Have you ever seen me give in?"

"Just the once."

I didn't need the reminder of that disaster. Coming off the ugly end of a long relationship, I'd plunged into another that had blown up in my face.

"Yeah, well, I learned my lesson. Don't date the students."

"Okay. You can stay," said Kim. "But you're due for a break. Why don't you head out back for a few minutes? Get some air."

I filled the latest order, avoided eye contact, and slipped through the door behind the bar. The back room was quieter, the music a muffled thumping from the other side of the wall. Heavy metal shelves lined the walls, and boxes full of liquor were stacked between me and the back door. The only light was the dim red flicker of the "Exit" sign and a thin wedge from the office.

I shivered as sweat dried in the cool air. Kim had left a pack of cigarettes on the edge of the desk. I could see them through the half-open door. I couldn't remember the last time I'd had a smoke. I decided now was a good time. My fingers trembled as I snitched a cigarette and a lighter.

Definitely a good time.

Navigating the maze of boxes, I opened the back door, intending to smoke in the alley.

Flares went off in my eyes, accompanied by the click and whine of cameras, like dozens of tiny machine guns. Voices roiled and spilled over me.

Something pushed me back into the storage room, and the door slammed shut with a bang. The noise faded, but big, spiky spots still danced before my eyes. I stumbled against a stack of boxes. The bottles in them rattled. A warm, strong hand grabbed my bare arm, keeping me from falling. The person reached past me to steady the boxes, and in that moment of contact, I knew it was a woman.

"Are you okay?" she asked. Her voice was breathy but deep, like a smoky lounge singer.

"I think so," I said. "What was that?"

"Paparazzi."

"I guess it makes sense with a goddess in the house."

"They follow her everywhere. There's more out front."

"I don't think our bouncer could handle that."

"He couldn't. Some of my sisters are up there helping."

The spots had mostly cleared away, and in the dim red glow of the "Exit" sign, I could make out my companion. She was about my height. She had a small nose, narrow chin, and eyes shadowed in darkness, so I couldn't tell what color they were.

"You're a priestess?"

"I am Alani."

"I'm Ben."

"Alani is a title. We're the hunting dogs of Artemis, her pack and protectors. My name is Jordan."

"I'm Ben. I think I said that already."

"You did."

"Sorry, I'm a little flustered. I just came back here for a smoke. I wasn't expecting the light show."

Jordan gestured towards a window set high in the wall.

"I could open that up, and you could smoke in here."

"I guess we're breaking so many laws already, one more won't matter."

She climbed on a stack of boxes and stretched towards the window. Jordan was slim and lean, with the body of an athlete or a martial artist. She wore jeans and a long-sleeved dark shirt. As she cracked the window, a flicker of flash bulbs gleamed off a silver necklace. Before the paparazzi realized no one was going to come climbing out and stopped shooting, I was able to tell that Jordan was probably in her mid-twenties—a little younger than me.

I moved over to help her off the boxes, but she jumped down unaided, landing lightly. Up close, I saw that the necklace was a crescent moon. She leaned against a shelf full of plastic cups and paper products and crossed her arms. I lit up.

"You work here?" she asked.

"I tend bar. I needed a break."

White teeth flashed in a smile.

"Smart move. It can get a little intense within the goddess's aura."

"I can only imagine it's worse up close. Does it get to you?"

"You get used to it," she said. "Being consecrated to her means you have a different relationship. Like a priestess, I'm still mortal, but I share in the divine, if that makes any sense."

"As much as anything about the gods does," I said. My hands were steadier now. "Consecrated to Artemis? What does that involve?"

"Ceremony," she said. "Commitment."

I knew that tone. That conversational path was closed to visitors—probably overgrown and thorny. I had some of those, too. I looked for safer territory.

"So what do you do when you're not keeping the paparazzi from sneaking in the back?"

"Travel with the goddess, hunt with her, dance with her, help her deal with the mortal world. I guess you could say we try to make sure that she's safe from mortals and they're safe from her."

"I can't imagine we pose much of a threat."

"More of a nuisance. A lot of what the alani do is ease the friction between Artemis and the mortal world. Priestesses lead the worship of the goddess. We manage the more mundane tasks."

"Like hunting? What's she hunting in Boston?"

"Nothing. We were in Maine before this, but she grew tired of the wilderness. Artemis leads the dance of the Muses and the Graces, too. For that, she needs music and people."

"I didn't know that."

"There's a lot people don't know about the gods. There's still a lot that I don't know."

Music rolled over us, accompanied by the roar of voices and the smell of sweat. Kim peered into the gloom from the half-open door.

"Ben? You about ready to come back?" she called. "Is there someone else back there?"

"It's okay," I said. "She's with the goddess. She's keeping the press out."

"Whatever the goddess wants. You coming? We could use your help."

"I gotta make a pit stop," I said, dropping my cigarette to the floor and grinding it out. "Then I'll be right there."

Kim closed the door, taking most of the noise with her.

"I guess you should get back," said Jordan.

Was that reluctance in her voice? That would be silly; we'd only just met. Of course, I wouldn't want to be stuck here, alone, guarding against the press while everyone else got to dance.

"Yeah. Can I get you a drink or anything?"

"Thanks, but I'm fine."

"Well, maybe I'll see you around."

"Maybe," she said. "I don't know how long the goddess will stay in Boston."

I opened the door. Light and noise spilled into the room. I glanced back. Stark shadows sprang from the boxes, and a rack of shelves cast bars of shadow across Jordan. She raised one hand in a gesture of farewell. I returned what I hoped was a jaunty wave.

The bar pulsed and throbbed, deafening after the relative silence of the storage room. A sea of women's faces greeted me from across the bar. Cassie, one of the other bartenders, gave me a friendly bump as she passed.

"Were you smoking?" she asked.

I ignored her. Even that little bit of contact had been enough to start me sweating again. I pushed out through the crowd to the men's room.

Farraday's men's room was little more than an overgrown closet with two urinals and a stall. Everything was painted a dark blue that you could barely see because of the advertisements for local bands and upcoming shows plastered all over—Stone Foundation, Fill & Kill, Zoey Rose, the Imp and the Mind Thing, and so on, a rainbow of hopefuls and has-beens. Every couple weeks, Kim sent one of us in to purge them.

I went straight to the stall. I have a bit of a shy bladder issue and prefer a closed door behind me. Besides, the advertisement for the urology clinic that hangs in front of one of the urinals weirds me out.

I was finishing up my business when the volume rose, and I heard two guys come in, laughing and talking.

"Oh my God," said one. "This is a mad house. Did you see the one in the corset?"

"No kidding man. That was crazy. Dave was lucky he brought his camera. He's gonna have awesome pictures."

"I bet he could sell them to some wild girls site or something. That much hotness in one room."

"He could definitely sell that one of the goddess."

"Dude, I think that's where he went. To sell it to one of the press guys up front."

"I wonder what a picture of a goddess's nipple is worth."

My stomach lurched as I thought of Los Angeles and angry gods. I zipped up. The door opened. Music and noise roared into the room, and they raised their voices.

"I don't know. That was so freakin' hot. I mean, I've seen some nice breasts before, but there's something about hers—"

I heard him say "they're not human" before the voices were lost in the crowd. I was already charging out of the bathroom, suffering a twinge of guilt as I passed the "All Employees Must Wash Hands" sign. Tonight was a night for rule-breaking.

In the narrow hallway outside the bathrooms, I ignored the line for the women's room and turned toward the bar. Two guys were merging with the crowd. I grabbed the shoulder of the one in the rear. He was a couple inches taller than me, skinny, with a shock of almost white hair. I grabbed hard, and he turned to bawl me out.

I'm not a big man, but I was fueled by fear and the strange energy that permeated Farraday's. I yanked him back and shoved him against the wall.

"What the—"

"Were you just in the bathroom?" I shouted.

"Yeah. Hey, aren't you the bartender?"

"Come with me."

I grabbed his arm. He resisted for a second then seemed to figure out I wasn't letting go. I dragged him behind the bar. Kim moved to block me. Her brow was furrowed, and she had a look that I knew meant she was going to start yelling. I held up a hand to forestall her.

"We have a problem. A big one. You gotta trust me."

She paused, mouth open, wheels spinning. Then she nodded and stepped out of the way.

I pushed the kid into the storage room, peering into the darkness.

"Jordan? You there? We've got trouble."

She materialized from the gloom. Her face was intent, focused.

"What is it?"

"Who the hell are you?" asked the kid. "What's going on?"

"Tell her what you said in the bathroom."

"Huh?"

"Your friend took a picture. Tell her about it."

"Oh. Dave had his digital camera and was just taking pictures, you know, of all the hotties."

"They took one of Artemis," I said.

"That's not such a big deal," said Jordan. "We don't want the press bothering her, but a mortal taking a picture is fine. It's a form of worship."

"It's not just that," said the kid. The gravity of the situation seemed finally to be sinking in. "It was a nip-slip."

"A what?" said Jordan.

"Her clothes moved, and he caught part or all of her nipple," I explained. "A wardrobe malfunction. There's whole web sites dedicated to that sort of thing."

Jordan cursed. "Where is this Dave? Where is the picture? And who else saw it?"

"He showed it to us guys at the table. Then he left. He's gonna sell it to one of the paparazzi. We figured it had to be worth a couple of grand."

"More like a couple of million," I said.

"More like his life and thousands more," said Jordan. "What does your friend look like?"

"A little shorter than me. About his height." He pointed at me. "But heavier. Brown hair, beard, and glasses. I think he's wearing a green shirt."

"Is he the one who always wears that stupid hat?" I asked.

"That's him."

"These guys are pretty regular. I know who he's talking about."

"Good." She turned on the kid. "I want you to listen to me very closely. You are in what can only be described as the deepest shit imaginable. When we get back to the bar, get everyone from your table and go out the back. Don't let any of the paparazzi in, get as far away as possible, and never speak of what you saw tonight. Do you understand?"

He nodded.

"Good. Because if Artemis learns of what you saw, nothing

on this earth that can protect you." She looked at me. "Come with me."

Then she was through the door. I half expected her to vault over the bar, but she just charged through Kim and Cassie. I heard glass breaking, but I ignored it and followed Jordan.

She cut straight across the dance floor. The lights were hot and the dancers hotter. I felt as if waves of energy were crashing against me. In seconds, I was soaked.

I kept my eyes focused on the thin line of hairs at the nape of Jordan's neck. Forceful but graceful, she picked up the rhythm of the crowd and slipped between sweat-soaked bodies almost as if dancing herself. I tried to stay in the clear space right behind her. A few times, I felt someone touch my arm or chest or back. Then I passed within arm's length of Artemis, and the rest of the world spun out of focus.

Her eyes were closed. She spun and gyrated, long limbs swaying like a tree in the wind. Her dark curls roiled like storm clouds, and the silver bangles caught and scattered the light. Artemis shuddered suddenly, head snapping up, cocked at an angle. Her eyes opened and met mine. I thought of a deer frozen in headlights. I wasn't sure if the image was her or me.

Something tugged at me, breaking the eye contact. Jordan had my arm. Her face was hard, eyes glittering. She mouthed, "Come on." I followed, leaving the goddess to her dance.

The front of Farraday's was a copy of the rear. As soon as we emerged, cameras clattered like typewriter keys. This time, I knew to shield my eyes from the flashes. Jordan tugged me to one side. She elbowed reporters out of the way, while other dark-clad young women pushed back the crowd. In a flurry of angry shouts and bruising impacts, we burst through the surrounding mob.

The restaurants, shops, and bars of Brighton Avenue spread in both directions. A Green Line train rattled down the middle of the street giving off a shower of sparks. Strolling party-goers wandered the sidewalks in packs—students roving from bar to bar. Rubberneckers stood in little clumps, trying to figure out why the crowd had gathered around Farraday's.

"Do you see him?" asked Jordan.

"No. The crowd's too thick."

She grabbed my hand. Before I could say anything, she'd jumped on the hood of a car. I clambered up, less gracefully. People stared and pointed. Some of the paparazzi turned and took pictures. Whatever happened was going to end up on the internet somewhere. I'd get my five minutes of fame.

Doing my best to ignore the flashes, I scanned the crowd.

"There!"

Jordan launched in the direction I pointed. She flew from the hood of the car, hitting the sidewalk without slowing. I'd watched greyhounds race once; she had that same grace.

I slipped while getting down, landed on my butt, and slid off the hood. Behind me, cameras flickered and flared against the night, lighting the street in lightning bursts. I crashed through the pedestrians, leaving angry couples in my wake, struggling to follow Jordan.

By the time I caught up with her, she'd cornered her quarry beside a parked S.U.V.

I recognized Dave. A local student and Farraday's regular, he was a slow drinker, a little overweight, and wore a fedora in the hope that it would lend him the appearance of coolness that he lacked. His companion wore jeans, a dark t-shirt, and a gray sport coat. He looked to be in his late thirties, and he was talking on his cell phone.

Jordan had already taken Dave's camera. She flipped it over, looked at the back, and then tossed it to me.

I juggled it like a hot potato, not wanting to see the screen.

"It's safe," said Jordan. "You won't see anything."

I looked. The screen read "No image available." I turned it over and popped the bottom open.

"The card's gone," I said.

"I tried to tell you," said Dave, pointing at his companion. "I sold it to him."

Jordan held out a hand to the man. "Give me the card."

He lowered the phone, seeming to notice us for the first time.

"You're one of her bitches, aren't you?" he said.

I lost it. High on adrenaline and the aura of a goddess, I punched him in the face. His attention was on Jordan, so he didn't see it coming at all. He staggered and dropped the phone. It skittered under the vehicle

"What the hell?" he said.

He lunged towards me, but Jordan was faster. She thrust out an arm to block him. Catching his shoulder with her free hand, she spun him around, grabbed his lapels, and slammed him up against the S.U.V.

"Where is the card?"

"Get your hands off me. She might be a goddess, but I'll have you for assault."

Jordan held him with one hand and searched the pockets of

his coat with the other.

"You have no idea what you're doing," she said. "That picture
—"

"—is worth millions."

"Millions!" whined Dave. "You paid me two grand."

Dave reached past Jordan, pawing at the man's coat. She backhanded him, and the blow sent him sprawling. He opened his mouth, but the words caught in his throat. He stared back towards Farraday's.

Artemis stood a few feet away. Alani flanked her—hard-eyed young women in dark clothing. Beyond them stood a ring of paparazzi. I realized they must have been there for a while, recording the whole exchange.

The goddess still held a drink in one hand, as if she hadn't really left the bar. In the bursting light of the flashes, away from the throbbing music and whirling dancers, she seemed smaller and more human. Inside Farraday's, she'd filled the room; up close, I could see that she was nearly a foot shorter than me.

"What is happening here, Jordan?" she asked in a voice like a bubbling stream.

"Nothing, my lady." Jordan looked down. "These men were causing trouble. I was dealing with it."

"I don't believe you're being completely honest with me," said the goddess.

She looked at me. Here eyes were dark, like the tree-covered slopes of ancient mountains. I was lost in those woods.

"It's a picture of you," I said, the words rising unbidden. "Your nipple is visible."

Jordan sighed and let go of the man. She took a step back.

"Hey," said the photographer. "It's a free country. You dress like that, you get photographed. Reasonable expectation of privacy and all that." He brushed at the lapels of his coat. "Is it worth something to you for me not to publish this? Call off your dogs and maybe we can work out a deal."

"I have not yet called my hounds," said Artemis.

"Good, then we can talk like civilized people."

Artemis laughed, a series of harsh, barks. I wondered why the man couldn't hear the rumble of thunder and the rising wind in her voice.

"There will be no talking. You are free to go. Both of you. Tell others now how you saw me—if you can."

Jordan grabbed me around the waist in a diving tackle that carried us both to the sidewalk. I dropped the camera. My elbow struck the pavement with bruising force.

Artemis flung her drink at Dave and the man. The liquid splashed them both. They wiped at their faces, spluttering.

Their pupils expanded, the darkness filling their eyes, even as their faces stretched. Dave clutched his head muttering "no, no, no" over and over again. The other man buckled over. Cloth tore as he bent. Tumors erupted from their foreheads. Black spears emerged between Dave's clutching fingers, branching and splitting to become horns. The man's neck stretched. The leather of his shoes split. His fists became hooves as they struck the sidewalk.

Two young stags stood in a pile of tattered clothing, frozen in the streetlight.

I lay on the ground. Jordan was on top of me. I could feel her warmth and strength, her breath on my neck. I felt myself responding to her touch.

She rolled quickly off me. Our eyes met briefly, and then she looked away.

"You okay?"

"Bruised but still human," I said. "Thanks."

"My pleasure."

Her eyes met mine again and held. I caught the hint of a smile.

Artemis raised a horn to her lips. I don't know where it came from, because she didn't have it in the bar. A low, deep, note sounded. The world receded. Traffic, people, music, all the sounds of the city faded away. Only the horn remained.

I felt a stirring in my heart, a flutter of fear, a call to flight. Jordan's face lit with expectation. She licked her lips.

The two stags bolted.

The doors of Farraday's burst open in a great roaring wave. Led by the two long-limbed athletes, the dancers scattered the paparazzi. A fierce cry of ecstasy rose from their mouths, like the baying of hounds, as they surged down the street after the fleeing stags.

Jordan looked at me. She was flushed, her eyes bright and eager. Her hair had fallen from its ponytail and hung about her face, wild and free.

"Ben," she said. "I have to go. Thanks. For trying to help."

"I'm sorry it didn't work out," I said.

"We stopped the picture from spreading," she said. "That's something."

Then she was gone, sprinting after the crowd, hair streaming, long limbs moving with leonine grace. A handful of alani ran with her. I watched until I lost her in the crowd.

I looked down at the pile of rags before me, flipping over a piece of torn, grey, pinstriped fabric. In what remained of the inside breast pocket, my fingers brushed a chip of plastic. I drew it out. Such a tiny thing.

I smelled pine needles, decay, and an animal musk. Artemis knelt beside me. Her long, delicate fingers closed on the photo card. They brushed against mine. The icy thrill of mountain waters coursed through my body. I felt cold and empty.

Artemis squeezed the card with her fingers, and it splintered. Fragments of plastic rained on the ground.

"Go back inside," she said. "This is not for you."

I didn't know if she meant the picture, the hunt, or Jordan. Neither did I care. The light in the goddess's eyes was cold and implacable as the moon.

When she stood, Artemis was no longer the dancer. She was the huntress. Nothing had changed and everything had. Barefoot, clothed in a shift of light, she bore a silver bow like a crescent moon in her hands. She was still the same size but seemed larger, as if she had somehow unwrapped herself.

I trembled, frozen. A soft voice whispered in my head, prayed that she wouldn't see me, that this time the hawk's shadow would pass over without harm.

Then Artemis, too, was gone, pursuing her hounds with a loping stride that carried her slender form through the crowd like a wolf through tall grass.

When she passed around the corner, the world crept cautiously back. The smells of exhaust, rotten garbage, and Chinese food came first. The sound of cars and music and a cackle of near-hysterical laughter came next.

Gradually, people shuffled back onto the sidewalk, went on about their evenings. A handful of the paparazzi ran towards the end of the block. They slowed as they reached the corner, looking around it almost reluctantly, making sure it was safe before continuing. Most remained where they were, scavengers unwilling to risk the attention of a true predator. A few of the lingerers snapped pictures of me as I walked back to Farraday's but most just moved out of my way. None of them followed me inside.

The bouncer crouched in the corner by the door. I don't think he recognized me. He wasn't really a tough guy, just a big man who traded on his size to earn some extra money at night. I couldn't imagine what it had been like when that mass of women poured through the door driven by the will of a goddess.

The bar was almost empty. No music played. Perhaps a dozen students—all male—were scattered about the dance floor. Some sat, some stood, some had their arms still raised as if to protect themselves. The lights cast shifting, flickering colors over their dull, slack-jawed faces. A dozen more hovered around the periphery, lingering nervously behind overturned furniture.

Some of the waitresses were already picking up chairs and bussing the tables, and Kim and Cassie were cleaning up behind the bar. Relief flooded Kim's sharp features as I met her eyes. She came around the bar and pulled me into a tight hug. We stood there for a long moment. At last, she pushed me away, searching my face.

"You okay, Ben?" she asked.

"I'm a little raggedy, but I'll survive."

"When the horn sounded, I thought—I don't know what I

thought. What happened out there?"

I thought for a moment—of pictures and moonlight and goddesses and Jordan. I gestured to the lost boys scattered around the bar.

"Let me help get this lot out of here. Then you can pour me a drink, and I'll tell you all about it."

"You sure?" she asked.

"I'm sure," I said. "It's an old story. It can wait a little bit longer."

William Gerke lives, works, and writes near Boston with his patient wife and their two ceaselessly-astonishing children. His short fiction has been published in Space and Time Magazine, Heroic Fantasy Quarterly, *and* Crossed Genres. *His first novel,* Endurance, *co-written with Meredith Watts, is available from No Downside Press (no-downside.com). You can learn more about William and follow his reading and writing life at williamgerke.com.*

Our Abstract World

KJ Kabza

Her opening at the MoMa was exquisite. I plugged the offered feeds into my brainjack and felt phantom textures: feathers, silk, wind, fur, oddly tactile sparkles.

I saw her in a corner, worked up some nerve, and approached her. I offered compliments.

"I want my art to make people feel something," she explained. "And in our increasingly immaterial, abstract world, we've forgotten the kind of pleasure tactile stimulation can bring."

"Some of us haven't forgotten." I hesitated. "...Would you like to get coffee sometime?"

A flutter of surprise vanished beneath her smile. She said, very gently, "I'm straight."

My smile matched hers. "That's a shame." Even in defeat— especially in defeat—you must be charming, and you must ignore whatever heat creeps into your ears.

She pointed to a feed in the corner. "Have you tried that one?"

My hot ears and I took the hint. I said no, thanked her

again, and left to go plug it in.

Phantom hands stroked my skin, half massage, half intimate invitation. "The artist used her own hands as the model," said the explanatory plaque.

I had to admit: this was one of the nicest defeats I'd ever experienced.

Sometimes our abstract world isn't so bad.

*For **KJ Kabza**'s bio, see* Sputnik 2, Interior, *p. 2.*

Graveyard Shift

David P. Fischer

"Love you, Mom. Talk to you soon."

"Oh, before I forget! I got a call from Silvia Kripke."

"You know it's weird that you talk to my exes, right?"

"I ran into her mother at the supermarket and gave her my card. Silvia's getting married and she hired me to do the planning!"

"Sudden bout of nausea. Gonna have to lie down on the floor now, Mom."

"Steve, don't be like that. She's a lovely girl. I'll never understand why things didn't work out with you two."

"I think it was related to the fact that she fled the country when I asked her to marry me."

"Steve, I would much rather be planning your wedding. Are you meeting people?"

"Goodnight, Mom. Love you."

Oof.

❦

A thump and a clear bell-like tone woke me from a dream. There had been an old man and an open cemetery gate, but the rest of the details slipped away. The thumping, however, continued. I looked out my window into the backyard and found my roommate, Calango, right on the other side of the pane. His arms were stretched toward me and he was visibly sweating. He turned and advanced in the other direction, striking and kicking the air to complete the form he was practicing. Somehow, said form took up fourteen and a half feet of space, while our backyard was fourteen feet and five inches. Calango's concession to this fact, if it could be called a concession, was to strike the outside wall of my bedroom with such force that it shook my bed and rang my alarm clock. Diplomacy around the issue had stagnated after a particularly biting comment regarding my luck at finally having some rocking in my bedroom on a regular basis. I watched Calango's retreating form and considered my day.

I had three patients in the morning, a long lunch, and a patient in the afternoon. The first patient wasn't for another three hours, leaving me plenty of time to contemplate my life.

I was unmarried with a nascent acupuncture practice, a crazed martial artist for a roommate, and a small aloe plant. The other occupant of my room had recently gone to the great fishbowl in the sky, and, thankfully, the aloe thrived on neglect.

Not exactly the life I had imagined. An image of Sylvia in a white dress flashed in my mind and went straight to my gut. My sudden bout of nausea returned. How was it the girl who left me because she didn't want to marry, because she never wanted to get married, was walking down the aisle before me?

I saw the dream again in my mind's eye. I knew what I had to do.

∽

There is a Tibetan practice. You walk in a graveyard at night every night until your fear becomes so palpable that it causes you to hallucinate. Your terror will then assemble itself into some sort of monstrous being. You offer yourself to it and it will eat you. If you're successful, you will be freed from fear forever. Like all spiritual practices, it carries its own variety of risks. According to Chinese medicine, fear attacks the kidneys, and abject terror can destroy them. The very spark of life is the energetic interplay between the right and left kidney. Those that fail in this meditation are at least conveniently located for the undertakers.

As a solution to my stuckness, it seemed obvious until I was walking toward the cemetery gates under cover of darkness. They were open, welcoming in theory, even at night. I came within a few feet of them and the tension in my chest was almost unbearable.

I turned around. Maybe I need to do this in stages, I thought. I kept walking and tried to focus on the positives. I had selected the Cambridge Cemetery in particular because it had open gates, vaultable fences and rolling hills. If the ground did decide to open up and start vomiting any sort of undead abomination, I figured the terrain would aid my escape. I also believed in my heart that I could clear its fences in one leap with a full head of steam from running down a hill.

Steeling myself, I stepped inside and felt a change the

instant I did, like walking into a soap bubble. Further into the cemetery, I began to feel a pressure at my lower back, kidney energy. Just as fear damages the kidneys, facing fear can nourish them. The graveyard meditation had already started to work its beneficial effects.

I was just starting to relax when I heard a noise. I froze. The same sound, closer. Footsteps! There was no wailing so I assumed it was a human being, and slowly turned to check. No one. Anywhere. It was nice to see that my mind was displaying such a can-do attitude when it came to playing tricks on me.

As I proceeded deeper into the cemetery, my thoughts began to drift. I wondered what advice those buried under me would give, what they would say if they could talk now. Aside, of course, from, "Braiiiins."

This was exactly the wrong frame of mind to be in when the footsteps returned. My heart started fluttering. I stopped moving. The sound came closer. I whirled. There was nothing. I stood frozen in place, when I saw a leaf drop slowly off a branch and land on the ground. It sounded like a human foot taking a step as it settled onto the other dried leaves. Autumn, the wrong season for graveyard walking.

My heart didn't quiet in my chest, and I decided that I wasn't constitutionally suited for the rigors of this particular meditation after all. I cut across a section of graves to head back to my car. Suddenly, I heard a voice. "I never should have—"

It cut off abruptly as I spun and looked around. No one. Okay, I was officially fed up with hearing things. Definitely time to go. I turned back towards my car and took a step. "I never should have sold the farm. The money helped, sure, but watching my kids grow up not seeing the stars broke my heart."

Just have to keep moving.

I took another few steps and heard, "Rebel, Union, it's all the same now."

I was almost back to the path and didn't want to give whatever forces were at work the satisfaction of seeing me break into a panicked run. I kept walking, more briskly. I heard, "I'm normally so good at identifying mushrooms."

I stopped and looked down. I was standing on a grave. I looked behind me and realized that each snippet of speech had come with treading upon someone's final resting place.

Leaving one foot on the grave of the failed mycologist, I stretched until I could put my other foot six feet above the dead soldier. For a moment their two narratives ran together. I heard other voices join one by one, then two by two, then with even greater frequency. The sound became an unintelligible cacophony, which suddenly transformed into hundreds of voices speaking clearly and in unison. "All flesh will pass, even yours!"

The shouted revelation hit me with the force of a physical blow, and I fell backwards onto the ground. Thankful I hadn't brained myself, I spent a moment looking up at the stars. Breathing heavily, I decided I'd made enough spiritual progress for one night. Taking care not to step on any more graves, I made my way to the exit.

I had parked below a burned out streetlight. When I opened the door, I remained in darkness. The interior light hadn't engaged. My heart sank but I tried to start the car anyway. Nothing. So much for a clean getaway.

I wrestled with my options. Sit for two hours waiting for Triple-A, or call Calango for a rescue. The increasing lateness of the hour had me dialing my roommate. I hoped the whole thing would be quick and painless, but past experience told me otherwise. Calling Calango would get me home earlier so I could get some sleep. Provided, of course, that we didn't end up across state lines on the run from Mounties, Federales, or some sort of combined expeditionary force. If I had learned anything from practicing various spiritual techniques, the late nights started to add up fast. If I had learned anything from rooming with Calango, there was no predicting the man.

Calango picked up and sounded fuzzy. "Steve? What time is it?"

"My car broke down."

"I am both asleep and not a mechanic."

"I know. I think I may just need a jump." I forestalled further comment by adding, "I'm only ten minutes away."

"Fine."

⌁

After the third failed jump, Calango removed the cables, made the sign of the cross over the hood, and began administering last rites.

"It's not necessarily dead," I objected.

"As far as tonight is concerned, it is." He opened his passenger door. "Get in."

I got in, and Calango said, "I want you to explain to me why I'm picking you up at cemetery in the dead of night."

"You like rescuing people?"

"Try again."

"I'm doing a meditation thing."

"Really? In a graveyard?"

"It's supposed to conquer fear."

"What are you so afraid of?"

I should have called Triple-A. "Nothing."

Calango turned off the car and pocketed his key.

I said, "Look. It's late. I'm tired."

"We are not going anywhere without the story."

"Fine. One of my exe's. She's getting married."

"Good for her. Since that news sent you into a tailspin, it seems like we're dealing with fear of dying alone here. What are you going to do about it?"

Calango restarted the car, and resumed driving.

The intense discomfort of the conversation reminded me that I was overdue for a cleaning and needed to call my dentist. If the car didn't stop at a light or something soon, maybe I could just unlock the door and dive out. If I tucked and rolled, I bet I would only end up with a scrape or two. Wait, did we just miss the turnoff to the house?

"I'm working on it!"

"In a graveyard? No, what you need is some genuine face to face interaction with real people."

Calango stopped the car. I looked around, preparing to escape. We were directly across the street from a bar.

Calango took the keys out of the ignition once again. "It's 12:30 AM and we're not going home until you get rejected by five women." He opened the door, and looked back at me. "And the same woman five times doesn't count. You'll meet a lot more girls in here than you will in a cemetery."

≪᳁

On the drive home, Calango was unduly satisfied with himself. I had had three conversations, resulting in two flat out noes and a phone number. Feeling he had made his point, Calango had let me slide on the final three rejections.

"She was nice too. What was her name again?"

"Alice."

"And pretty."

"She's also moving to another city for work."

"In like a month! Man, it's like there's no hope for you. You'd rather lurk in a graveyard than be on a date with a beautiful woman."

I sighed. I wasn't sure he was entirely wrong.

≪᳁

The next night, Calango walked in to find me on the couch. "Car fixed?"

"Yup."

"It's 10:45. Shouldn't you be out doing your fear thing?"

"Last night's graveyard experience was pretty intense, I'm taking a moment to reflect."

Calango sat down next to me. He said gently, "Steve, you know how I feel about cowardice."

"What?"

"The cemetery meditation is a cop out, but it's at least a feeble attempt to maybe, one day, face your demons."

I turned toward him, not liking the direction the

conversation was going.

He put a sympathetic arm around my shoulder and asked, "Are you afraid of returning to the graveyard?"

"I'm not scared, I just—"

Calango cut me off by swiftly grabbing me around the neck and upper body. The next thing I knew, I was outside on my back. I tried the front door. It was locked. I reached into my pocket and discovered my keys were gone. Left without options, I rang the bell. Calango answered using the intercom.

"Yes?"

"This is not okay. Let me in."

"Bring back a nice interior shot of the cemetery if you want to get into the house."

The intercom shut off, and I heard a metallic clink. My car keys, separated from my keychain, landed in front of me as Calango grimly shut the front window.

I never should have let him get that close.

Graveyard, night two. I left my car, made sure all the lights were off, and walked up the street to the cemetery. I braced myself and entered. After I was deep into the center, I took out my phone and snapped a photo of a large crypt. Then I hopped from side to side trying to get the momentum necessary to step on another grave. I cringed and put my foot down. Nothing. No voices, no sensation. Confused, I stretched out my other foot and placed it on a different plot. Still nothing. Maybe last night's adventure had been the work of an overactive imagination.

A thin mist began to seep out of the ground. And here I had

thought it couldn't get any creepier than a chorus of dead people telling me I was going to join them.

I got off the graves and the mist thickened. I moved forward. The temperature dropped with each step until I could see my breath, and I broke out in shivers. If I survived the fear monster only to be felled by the cold, I was going to be very upset.

The mist became a waist-high fog, and I was beginning to have trouble navigating. I tried to rely on trees and signposts to keep me from barking my shins on the headstones of dearly departed.

After about ten minutes, the fog finally worked its way up to the level of my head. I couldn't see more than two feet in any direction, and was beginning to worry about how I was going to find the exit, much less complete the meditation. Graves loomed and slowly resolved as I passed them. One directly in front of me had an odd shape that drew my eye. Still shaking, I got closer. It was a heart superimposed on a rectangle. In the center it read, *Love*.

Another headstone came into view in front of me. It was inscribed with the words, *Get Out of My Car, Steve*.

A conversation, or part of one. Prom night 1995. Valerie Hutchins had been unwilling to tolerate the fact I had not quite been ready to sleep with her. I had had to walk down from the hills and catch the bus home.

I continued toward the exit. Another grave. *I Don't Understand Why It Has To Be This Way*.

Melanie Ruiz, 1996. I supplied the rest of the conversation in my head.

"Look we're both going away to school. Name one couple we know that has survived more than six months after that," I said.

Melanie replied, "Don't you love me? Isn't one more day, one more month, one more year better than ending it all right now?"

"Can't we just be realistic? If we break up now it will be less painful than waiting to do it at Thanksgiving."

The sound of her tears had returned to me in quiet moments throughout freshman year.

I stopped and spun in a circle. *Burn Every Photo You Have Of Us And Never Think Of Me Again.*

Sayako Sato, 2005.

She had been my most serious girlfriend. After two years together, she had taken a friend of mine home with her following a late night party. I had been studying abroad in China, and thinking about proposing. Unbidden, the dialogue flooded back.

"Steve, I never meant to hurt you."

"What exactly did you mean to do!?"

"I was lonely. I was drunk. It only happened once."

"I can't believe you did this to me."

"I told you right away. I could have kept it secret."

"Do you want bonus points for that?"

"I want to know you'll be okay. I can't undo what happened but I want to make it right."

"I want you to understand that I will never forgive you. Burn every photo you have of us and never think of me again."

The next day, I realized exactly how far away I had been twisted from who I wanted to be.

Even now, I felt tears of shame welling up and wondered if this was the final stage of the meditation, where it was revealed that I had been wholly consumed by a monster long, long ago.

I stood up to get a better view, and the fog cleared completely, taking the tombstones with it. After a moment of shock, I shouted, "What?!"

As my voice echoed back to me, I realized now might be an excellent time to leave.

∽

The next night I returned to the graveyard. The instant I parked, a heavy rain started.

I sat in my car and cursed the unpredictability of New England weather, until I remembered that that same unpredictability had led me to store a rain jacket and umbrella in my trunk. Then, I spent a moment cursing my foresight. Forty minutes of rain in a pitch dark cemetery did not seem like a prescription for fun.

I decided to gear up and pass through the gates. If I didn't feel anything, I would turn around and hope for better weather tomorrow.

My clothes almost got soaked through in the time it took to walk to the back of the car and find my umbrella. I shrugged the jacket on, alternating the closed umbrella between hands. The instant I opened the umbrella the rain transformed into a deluge that made the word torrential seem inadequate. I felt water seep into my shoes and consoled myself that at least there was no wind.

I walked forward and rounded the corner. Vision obscured by the weather, I felt it in my body the instant I entered the cemetery. The pressure at my lower back was almost unbearable. Tonight was the night, all right.

❦

I was in the middle of my circuit when mist started rising from the ground. My back felt like the bones were going to crack and I bent over to get some relief. In the distance, swirling mists parted to reveal a female form. I took a small penlight out of my pocket and tried to get a better view. The figure held an umbrella in one hand and a lit cigarette in the other. She appeared to be human, although keeping tobacco lit in this weather was an almost supernatural feat. She paused, took a drag on her cigarette, and came close enough to call out. "Hey there, flashlight, want to help a damsel in distress?"

Uncertain, I asked, "Are you a metaphor?"

"Look, I'll be a hyperbolic simile if you'll help me fix my flat."

"Your flat?"

"I need you to hold the light while I change my tire."

"This is not what I expected."

"I'm sorry, flashlight, is your late night graveyard walk not living up to your expectations?"

"My name is Steve."

"Steve, I need your help."

I followed her out of the cemetery.

❦

"After I broke down, I realized it was too dark to get anything done without being soaked to the bone." She handed me the jack. "I set off through the cemetery because it looked like the best way to get to civilization. Lucky I found the groundskeeper!"

Now, we got to the especially embarrassing portion of the evening. "I'm not the groundskeeper."

She looked at me. I tried to appear nonthreatening.

She said slowly, "What brought you to the cemetery then, Steve?"

"I was doing a meditation thing." I placed the jack under the car and began to crank.

Dissatisfied with my effort, she edged me out of the way and reset the jack. Then, she handed me her flashlight.

"In a graveyard? Like a mortality, acceptance of death thing?"

"With a facing fear component."

"I knew that comparative religions course would come in handy. Well, thanks for taking the time to help."

"No problem. Wait, I can unscrew the bolts."

"You're already helping a whole lot holding the light and umbrella. Just worry about keeping me dry, lit and entertained."

"I really think—"

"Steve, the way you handled that jack told me you're not much of a gearhead. I've changed my share of tires. We'll be done soon enough."

"You win. What's your name, by the way?

"Calliope."

"Nice to meet you." I paused. "Calliope?"

"Mama was a classics major."

"I see."

"What about you, Steve? What's your story?"

"I practice acupuncture and help people change tires in

bad weather."

"Funny. You married?"

"No."

"Ah, still enjoying single life?"

"Not really, no."

"Do you mean you have a girlfriend?"

"No."

"Then, what?"

"I'm taking a break."

"Are you shy?"

"No. I—"

"Gay?"

"No."

"What then?"

What the heck? I decided. "I feel badly about some things I've done, about some things that have been done to me. I think I need to heal before—"

She turned and looked up at me. "Before what?"

"I—"

"Steve, how are you supposed to have positive, healing experiences if the bad ones keep you hiding at home?"

She had started to gesture at me with the tire iron and I became concerned that she might try to use it to beat some sense into me. I relaxed when she returned her attention to the spare.

"There are things I need to get through first."

She grimly clutched the tire iron and shook her head. She turned and began to stand up. She seemed incensed.

I got nervous. This was usually how they killed drifters in movies. I opened my mouth, and Calliope silenced me with a kiss. Tender, but the shock nearly killed me.

"Tire's fixed."

"Uh, do you want to—"

"You're sweet, but you're not paying attention. I've got places I need to be. You just needed inspiring."

She gave me a hug. When she squeezed, I could hear pops and cracks as my spine realigned itself. The pressure at my back disappeared and I felt like I had gained two inches in height.

She held me and murmured into my chest. "Driving the joy out of your life is like committing suicide without killing yourself. I don't know who you think you owe, or what kind of penance you're trying to pay, but life's for living. Fully."

She poked me in the chest, leaving an electric shock that travelled to my lungs. Then, she walked to the driver's side of her car. Somehow, the flat had gotten into her trunk.

"What—" I began.

She kept going. "Thanks again, Steve. You take care ... and think about what I said."

I nodded and watched her drive off into the night. Even after the rain stopped, I resisted the impulse to search for a grave with her name on it.

As soon as I got home, Calango asked, "Did it work?"

"More or less."

"How do you feel?"

"Wet and cold."

I headed towards my room and he called after me, "Are you free from fear?"

I turned back, smiled, and said, "No."

The next morning I remembered something I had to do. I took out my phone and dialed a number.

It rang once, twice. Then, the line connected.

"Alice? It's Steve. We met the other night..."

David P. Fischer practices acupuncture and teaches martial arts in the Greater Boston area. He is graduated as a professor of Capoeira Angola under Mestre Deraldo Ferreira with over 16 years experience. In addition, he traveled to China in 2008 and 2011 to study Pi Gua Zhang, Body Hardening, Tiger Hooks, and Crazy Demon Staff with the late Master Zhou Jing Xuan. He has studied Kalaripayattu and Nayak Family Healing Yoga with Guru Pradhuman Nayak for over 5 years. He has practiced qi gong for the past 17 years, and studies meditative traditions from around the world. In 2015, after years of intensive study, he was able to reconstruct the lost alchemical tradition of the Eight Vessel Scripture, a form of meditation last practiced during the Ming Dynasty.

David is a licensed acupuncturist and herbalist with a Masters degree from the New England School of Acupuncture, a BA in East Asian Studies from Brown University and, unexpectedly enough, an MBA from Babson College. You can find out more about David Fischer, his fiction, and his travels at www.evilspiritstremble.com.

Sweet Dreams

Meredith Watts

I'd first like to apologize. I am not human. I am a supernatural being. And, well, there is no Match.com for us. Guess we're supposed to have that soulmate thing taken care of already.

Scratch that. Horrible way to begin.

I have traveled the world. I enjoy surprises, music, dancing, dreams. I really like dreams. I am looking for someone with an open mind, who can adapt to last minute changes in plans and who is very accepting of others, different lifestyles and different life experiences. Very different.

Desperate.

My name is Baku, and I'd like to be the one for you.

Ugh. Enough with profiles. Maybe something easier?

Gender: Male? Female? Transsexual Person? Agender? Bigender? Androgynous?

There wasn't an "otherworldly being" option, was there?

∾

Annie doesn't know why she is here. It's not her scene, not what she typically does. She's an office drone. The highlight of her existence is collating papers in one of the fancy conference rooms. The most outrageous thing she's ever done is spend a week up to her shins in muck volunteering on a dairy farm.

A crowded club in the sketchy part of town is so far outside of her comfort zone that she'd need a GPS to find her way back. Music thumps through speakers: a steady, driving beat that shakes her brain in her skull and rattles her heart in her chest. The lights strobe and probe across the room, casting the crowded scene in shocks of color and shadow.

She blocks the blinding light with her hand. Her strapless dress shifts. With a frown and a squint, she hikes it up in front.

"What brought you here tonight?"

Yeah. That is the question of the evening. Why did she come? She couldn't sleep. After tossing and turning and fighting with her dreams she got out of bed and was struck by a thought—an impulsive thought—and something made her give in. She'd driven by this place countless times and tonight, this night, she came.

Wait, someone spoke to her. She looks around for the source

of the voice. She's surrounded by people, but no one sees her. Just like at her work and with her family. She is with a crowd and yet not part of it at all.

Strange. This place was supposed to be different.

Circulate through the crowd. Don't give people everything they need, but don't leave them so lacking that the fantasy seems unattainable.

Above all else, stay focused. Don't let the mind wander. Don't think about that silly dating profile.

I suppose I should explain why I am trying to find companionship—specifically human companionship. My kind don't get lonely. We're not supposed to, anyway. We have the purpose we are designed for. Beyond that... Well, there isn't supposed to be a beyond that.

Come on, focus. Be the center of everything, this is your court. There's one looking to be conquered. This one wants a man. That one wants a woman. Another wants to be worshipped. Everyone is looking for something.

I can't even say for certain what I want. To be seen as more than what I am? To be seen at all? I've had one purpose for an eternity. I'm tired. I want something different.

Be the unattainable. Humans dream. Humans dream of sugary futures, of sharp risk, of transcendent and terrible desires.

I'm so tired of sweet. I'm so tired of the edge. I'm so tired of the nightly chase and the ritualistic culmination of someone else's dream.

No luck. The dating profile crowded out all else. It had for weeks now.

"So tell me, sweet maiden," says the artwork of androgyny. The barely whispered words caress her as they ply the space between masculine and feminine. "Just who do I have the honor of buying a drink for?"

"I'm Annie."

"Not your name. Names are so restrictive." Her admirer whispers, yet over the sound of the driving bass and cacophony of conversations she can hear every word. The voice feels closer to her than the sheets she sleeps under at night. "Who do you want to be?"

She stares at the person so very different from everything she knows. She can't determine anything. Age, height, gender. It all seems variable. Her admirer stands at least a foot taller than her or is maybe her height. Short orange hair, flat-chested and broad-shouldered with an hourglass figure and well dressed in what looks like a cross between a tux and an evening gown.

"I know you," she says.

"Everyone knows me," says her admirer. "And no one does."

She shakes her head. That seems right but wrong. "I swear we've met before."

Lips and eyelids gleam in the black light that bathes the dance floor. The open neck of a shirt plunges to the bottom of a bare sternum. Pants hug slim hips.

Her admirer smiles with eyes that take her in and the air around her. "Ah, yes. I see it now. I should have known when I saw the light in your eyes."

"Known what?"

"We have met before. You've dreamed about me."

She knows this to be true. She has dreamed of this person. Those dreams brought her here. Her head spins from the rush, from the attention, from the anticipation. "Who are you?"

Her admirer leans in close. A smooth cheek brushes against hers. It smells like sandalwood and lilies. "I am the cultivator and consumer of wayward dreams."

She laughs. "What does that mean?"

They stand so close that she starts to wonder whether she's feeling the beat of the music or the beat of another's heart.

"I own this place," her admirer says. She feels warm breath against her neck.

A shiver of pleasure snakes down her spine. "You're Baku? Baku Tapir?"

They start with easy questions. The ones that are no problem to answer.

Name: Baku Tapir
Occupation: Owner, Baku's Back Alley
Height: However tall you want me to be

Hair Color: See above
Eye Color: See above
Age: How rude of you to ask!
Profile: ...

That was the troublesome part. Describe the being that is what everyone else wants them to be. A being that didn't even have a name.

Okay, so Baku Tapir isn't exactly my given name. It's the name I gave myself, which is a mix of the designations or purposes I was given, but it has become me inasmuch as anything could be me.

No preferences. No tastes. No identities. Inclinations... maybe.

Some of my brethren like to nurture political dreams. Some like dreams of power. Some like dreams of peace and quiet and some like dreams of darkness and torment.

I like dreams of romance. I like dreams of love and passion and desire. And yet I'd give anything to be with someone who would be content to spend a quiet evening alone together dressed in comfortable clothes doing whatever feels right.

The problem is that the patrons at Baku's Back Alley see the mysterious bar's owner and dream of sex and lust and infinite nights filled with risk and pleasure to distract them from the reality of their lives.

Back to work.

❧

The bartender hands Baku a martini glass filled with a dark, frothy, glittery liquid. It swirls in its conical cage, a galaxy of eddies and vortexes and stars being born.

Baku presents it to her. "To officially welcome you to Baku's Back Alley, I give you Dare to Dream."

She takes the glass. Her gut tells her not to hesitate. Her heart says to trust, that this stranger is a friend, she just doesn't realize it yet.

She sips the drink and swoons. Cold and warm, sweet with a hint of tart. She tastes true love wrapped in a package called lust. She tastes art, the purity of creating something from nothing. She tastes the bittersweet that comes from reaching for something you know you'll never attain, but by God, that's not going to stop you from trying.

She stares with wonder into the depths of her glass. "What's in it?"

"Imaginings. Fantasies. Desires. With a dash of gold flakes and enough saké to knock your soul free from your body." Baku's hand caresses her waist and every part of her lights up.

Baku smiles wistfully as she abandons decorum and empties the glass, licking her lips to get every last drop, then Baku takes her face in warm hands and kisses her. Her heart flutters. She feels herself rising. Her body stretches to reach up to Baku's. Air shudders in her lungs, choked out by desire. She struggles to breathe.

What if every night could be like this? Ending in a haze of top-shelf transgressions? Her lips curl in a smile.

What if every day could be like this? Would Baku be the man

of the house or the woman? She imagines a person dressed in a business suit and heels, vacuuming the living room and drinking a beer.

"You're glowing," Baku says with delight. Grabbing her hand, Baku leads her onto the dance floor. The other dancers watch them pass with hunger in their eyes.

That's right. Be jealous! She wants to tell them. She is the target of Baku's attentions. Baku Tapir! The trophy. The ultimate prize. She licks her lips and tastes velvet smugness and the tiniest trickle of shame.

Baku twirls her to the middle of the floor and nods to the DJ. The music gracefully shifts from a hard driving dance beat to a slower, sultry samba.

She is dancing with a mysterious stranger, a person she knows nothing about. Christ, she can't even be sure of their gender. This should feel strange and dangerous, but to her it feels right. It feels normal. She doesn't know why people should feel jealous anymore. She's not doing anything out of the ordinary. She's just doing what comes naturally, what they could and can and actually do with the people they are with.

She's known Baku forever. There is no pedestal raising this person above the masses. Well, maybe there was, but now she is on the pedestal too and the extraordinary had become delightfully commonplace.

"Tell me," Baku whispers, hips and hands moving freely against her. "What happens next?"

She closes her eyes and dreams. "I let myself go crazy. You take me somewhere we can be alone and show me yourself in a way you've never shown anyone else. You blow my mind."

I don't sleep with the people who come to my club. Not really. That I am a conqueror—that there are conquests—is one of the wilder rumors that swirl around me. I mean, they think they do, but it's a fantasy like the dreams I help them create. It's part of the dream. It's not real. Not like what I'm after at all.

Sex, sex, sex. It always comes back to sex. Why can't it be something else for a change? Why does no one dream of sea creatures or yesterday's fashions or purple cows? What are people afraid of?

"Is that all?"

Baku dips her. She tenses and opens her eyes for a moment to regain her sense of balance. All the other patrons are standing around them, staring; their eyes, even hungrier than they were before. Their eyes devour.

Her tension doesn't go away. She turns her head this way and that, keeping her eyes on theirs, on them.

"Baku, why are—"

"Shh... you're imagining things," the voice says breathlessly.

Glass crunches beneath her boot. She takes her eyes off the others for a moment and glances down. Oh God. Not glass, but a hypodermic syringe. The needle glints like a spine from a sea urchin.

What the hell?

She looks up and the patrons are no longer human. Eyes

that stared with lust now gape with predatory malice. The whites have drowned in the blackness of endless throats. Eyelashes thicken and glint like fangs. Faces stretch and elongate, their once human mouths open and scream soundlessly as their transformation tears them apart. Their bodies break and break and break along to the beat of music. Their bones turn to dust as they melt into limp and flailing grotesques.

She faces Baku. That exquisite body blurs. Oh God, what is it? She doesn't wait to find out. She runs for the door. Dancers tangle her legs with their formless limbs. She trips over their fleshy bodies, feels their fangs scrape against her skin. She drags herself away, scrambling on all fours.

The door shuts behind her with an ominous thud, plunging her into near darkness. She regains her footing and backs away, staggering down the alley that led her there. Her feet echo hollowly on a metal grate. Sewage rushes beneath her. The water froths like blood in the bathtub of a slasher flick. Baku's Back Alley looms before her like a serial killer, a monstrosity of steel and concrete, mortar and grit with no windows and one heavy door that looks like it was stolen from a medieval fortress.

She doesn't remember it looking this way when she came in.

Her heart hammers in her chest. Breath rips through her lungs. Black light casts everything in an eerie glow.

The alley wasn't lit this way before.

"Because you're not in the alley," Baku whispers. "You're still inside."

Her eyes widen. She spins to find the voice and the world spins with her. She is blinded and terrified, as small as a mouse before a cat.

She looks down at herself. She doesn't have hands or feet.

Pink paws scramble across the floor. Brown fur covers her body. Her face stretches in the blink of an eye. Her knees break and bend backward.

And she is glowing.

"The glow around you... It's your dreams," Baku says.

Baku kneels before her, form still a blur. Hands and feet turn into tiger paws. Arms and legs bloom orange, rippling with black stripes. Baku's body thickens and yellows, golden fur spreading over it. A tufted tail whips about. Orange hair engulfs head and neck in a luxurious mane. Horse ears flick about wildly. Mouth and nose merge and stretch. Lower canines sharpen and burst into tusks. A prehensile nose like a brown furred elephant trunk reaches for her.

She closes her eyes and pulls away. She screams but only a strange squeaking emerges from her mouth.

This is how she is going to die. The club-goers will laugh at her passing and say that she died as she lived: passively and in passive voice.

No. She refuses. She forces her eyes open.

Above all else, stay focused. Don't let the mind wander.

I am a (_____) seeking a (_____) and I'm very sorry.

The elephant-trunked beast stands before her. She backs away crab-like until she bumps into a wall. Her body shakes. She stares at her hands, her human hands, expecting crab claws to form at any second, but nothing happens.

"Don't worry. The nightmares are gone now," Baku says.

She feels every part of herself to check that she is in fact herself. Nothing is bleeding. She's whole, and the club is empty and silent. No more gaping grotesques. No more music. No more anyone. She is sitting in the corner at the edge of a pool of dusty white stage light. She can see every corner of the club: the lights hanging above her, the tables and chairs upstairs, the scuffs on the floor, the brick walls. It looks plain and ordinary, like a black box theater after the show has been struck. It smells a little musty, like a house with a perpetually damp basement. There's something homey about it.

She'd be willing to believe that she'd been rufied or had just come down from the highest trip of her life, that it had all been a hallucination, except for the strange tiger-lion-elephant creature that stands before her.

Baku groans and lies on the floor, his stomach, uncomfortably swollen. If his eyes weren't so big and brown and wincing in pain, she would have run away, but there's vulnerability about him that she can't turn away from.

"What the hell happened to me?"

"I was hungry and you looked very appetizing." The voice emanates from him and wraps around her, like his whispers had done.

She gapes. "You *ate* me?"

"Your dreams, honey. I only ate your dreams. It's what I do." The soft brown eyes gaze into hers. She wasn't scared. She wasn't sure what she was. "They looked like they were going to be unrealized *petit fours*—pretty and palatable. But my mind was elsewhere. You must have felt me feeding and the little dream *amuse-bouches* became a platter of nightmares." His prehensile nose points toward the bar. "Nightmares give me heartburn like you wouldn't believe, and yours... Well, yours were the greasy breakfast after last call—fatty, salty, and binge-worthy. There's some alka-seltzer under the counter. Do you mind?"

"I do, actually."

He groans again. She watches as his form blurs and morphs, flattening herself against the wall, expecting the horrible beasts to return. Instead, the person named Baku as she more or less knew him emerges from the transformation. His orange hair is dank and lifeless. Dark circles threaten to eat his eyes. His face is as puffy as a sorority girl's after rush week. But he's not entirely who she remembers him being. His arms are faintly tiger striped and a tail hangs defeated between his legs. He is wearing a plain tunic that drapes to his knees and no pants. His gut pushes against the seams. He looks like he sat down to Thanksgiving dinner and ate everyone's share.

Shaking, he stands and drags himself to the bar, shielding his eyes from the light. He sits on the bar and fumbles underneath. Annie watches silently as he plops two alka-seltzer into a glass and barely waits for the fizz to begin before guzzling it all.

"The things you dream up don't go down well." His voice is thick, deeper than it was before, but still neither male nor female.

She runs her hands through her hair. "I must still be high."

By the unpleasant twisting of his features, she can tell that some of what he ate was coming back up. He slumps sideways, curling into a fetal position. He looks awkward and terrible and vulnerable.

"You weren't high," he grumbles. "I just gave you something to make your dreams more vivid and easier for me to eat."

"Are you really comfortable like that?" she asks.

"No." He rolls off the bar and starts to plod toward a door in the back. "I'm going to have to close the club for at least a week while I wait for these nightmares to pass. You can imagine how much fun that will be." He grimaces. "Actually, don't imagine it at all. I've seen what you come up with."

She winces sympathetically. He just looks so miserable.

"It's not your fault. I'm sorry I frightened you."

"You don't frighten me. Apparently I frighten me."

Baku's stomach burbles. "You'll forget it all, don't worry."

"What?"

"The nightmare. The memories will fade. You'll forget. There's nothing to remember, really. I ate them. As for me like this, you'll forget that too. Or, at least, you'll think it was only a dream."

Annie scowls. "No. I want to remember."

"No human has ever seen me like this before." Baku pauses, leaning on the door frame. More burbles emerge from his gut, followed by an involuntary venting. He blushes. "Why would you want to remember this?"

He disappears into the back. Annie stumbles after him. Her dress slows her down. She catches herself on the door frame. The wood is still warm where he touched it.

"Because it's the most honest thing that's ever happened to me."

Who could disagree with that?

I am a dream eater seeking honest companionship. Accept me as I am or not at all.

≈6

The back room turns out to be a small, quaint studio apartment. The kitchen feels about a decade old. The living room has a fairly large bookshelf and a well-loved tan sofa. Everything about the place is perfectly normal. Except the bed. The bed looks like something Rudyard Kipling would dream up with a few modern touches. It has palm fronds and branches, soft grasses and leaves. There are bits of flannel sheeting, down pillows and memory foam draped in mosquito netting with surround sound.

"You sleep here?"

He gives her a sidelong look, then says, "I'm a tapir," as though that clears everything up.

"I thought you said you're Baku."

"Baku, tapir, what's a label between friends?"

She starts. "Friends?"

His shoulders droop at the question. He flops himself into the nest of leaves and foam and feathers. His stomach contents slosh, and he groans.

"There're some clothes in the closet over there," he says with a half-hearted wave.

"You're letting me wear your clothes?"

"Seems fair. Take what you want. You don't look comfortable in that outfit."

"I'm not." She adjusts the dress, but it's still pinching and scratching at her. "The tag has been digging into my side all evening."

She goes to the closet. There are evening gowns next to tuxes next to jeans and shorts and skirts. She grabs a t-shirt and a pair of yoga pants. She doesn't know where to change and glances at Baku. He turns away. Annie strips out of the cocktail dress and slides into Baku's clothes. They fit nicely. Maybe he is about her height. It's so hard to tell. But they're well-worn and soft and clean but still smell a bit like sandalwood and lilacs. Like him … like her?

She smiles. Yes, friends. She feels strangely comfortable here in his home and in his clothes, like they've been friends forever.

When she looks back at Baku, his form is blurring. She studies the wall in front of her. It just seems polite not to watch someone change.

"Do me a favor before you go?" he says. "Just hit play on that remote."

On top of a speaker she finds a slim, black remote control. She picks it up and hits play. A smooth song with deep female vocals wafts through the air.

"I know this song," she says. "I like 80s music."

Baku's transformation is complete. Tiger legs stretch out from a cuddly lion body. A tired tail flicks absentmindedly. A short, elephant nose emerges from a tusked, horsy face. His brown-furred muzzle stretches open in a giant yawn as he settles into the strange bed.

After a few minutes all she hears is the sound of deep breathing. Baku's chest slowly rises and falls. His feet kick a few times as he drifts off sleep.

Is this when she goes back home? What more is there to do?

Just one thing.

She smiles as she steps over a few branches and climbs into Baku's bed. He stirs and wiggles to make room for her. She hears his heart beat and the burbling of his belly as she snuggles into his soft, warm fur and rests her head against his chest.

"Sweet dreams," she whispers as she drifts off to sleep.

She has snuggled close. Her sleep will be dreamless, which is fine for now. It is enough just to feel her warmth.

Maybe I don't need this personal ad after all.

Meredith Watts *lives near Boston with her overly energetic dog, Zoe. Her day job involves a frightening amount of numbers. She is grateful for writing where anything frightening is fantastical rather than numerical in nature. She also has a propensity for climbing high into the air, wrapping a bit of fabric around herself and swan diving towards the floor, and readily admits that her concept of what's frightening is might be slightly off from center. She has a short fiction piece in the first* Pen-Ultimate *anthology. Her first novel,* Endurance, *co-written with William Gerke, is available from No Downside Press (no-downside.com).*

Spira Mirabilis

Orin Kornblit

"Daddy, am I going to die?"

I look down at my young son, nestled in his bed, and wonder how I'm going to answer him. The sounds of the guests downstairs drift up as a gentle murmur, punctuated by occasional bursts of laughter.

I see the anxiety in his little face and try to remember my first awareness of mortality. I decide to give him the simple truth.

"Someday you will, Timothy. But not for a long time."

"I'm scared. I don't want to die."

"I know. No one wants to, but it happens to everyone eventually. It's part of growing up. We all have to take turns being children, then grown-ups, then hopefully, parents and grandparents. After that we have to leave to make room for other people to be born."

"Are you scared?"

"Sometimes. I try and remind myself that I'm not alone, that it happens to everybody, and that I shouldn't waste time worrying about it because there's nothing I can do."

My little boy regards me quietly. I can see calm begin to settle around his eyes.

"Does that help?" I ask.

"Yeah. I think it does. Thanks, Dad."

I run a hand through his hair and give him a kiss on his forehead. I make sure the nightlight is on before turning out his lamp and leave the door open a hand's-breadth behind me as I go.

As I make my way down the stairs, I catch snatches of conversation. I can hear Mrs. Sloan quoting from the Bible, of all things.

"... And all the days that Adam lived were nine hundred and thirty years; and he died. And Seth lived a hundred and five years, and begot Enosh. And Seth lived after he begot Enosh eight hundred and seven years ..."

"That's ridiculous." My wife's voice. "People never lived that long."

By now I'm downstairs and can see our friends shifting uncomfortably. My old school buddy, Bob Sloan, is standing behind his wife's chair with a look of apologetic embarrassment on his face.

"Maybe they did." Edith Sloan's voice is quivering. "Maybe they did, once. But then God punished them for their wickedness."

I sit down on the couch next to my wife. Joanne takes my hand in hers and gives it a gentle squeeze. I look at her profile and fall in love all over again. The touch of gray in her hair and first signs of wrinkles have not diminished her beauty. Rather, they have given her an air of authority. She's not a woman to cross lightly.

"And you think we are being punished for our wickedness, is that it?" she asks.

"What else? What else could it be?" Edith's voice chokes

with emotion and her gaze drops to the floor.

The crowd devolves into murmuring groups, each with their own answer. She's right. She's crazy. We should look to religion. To science. It's because of global warming, or CO_2 levels, or industrial pollution. The discordant chatter and Bible talk makes me think of the story of Babel.

Mrs. Sloan is being comforted by her husband. Embarrassed by her outburst, she's wiping tears from her eyes and hiding behind a cadaverous smile.

My boss, Dr. Collins, delicately makes his way toward us, leaning on his cane. "How is that boy of yours doing? All tucked in?"

"Yes, Timothy's fine." I think about the conversation upstairs. I had hoped to preserve his innocence a little longer. "They grow up so fast."

"So true. Ever think about having more?"

"We'd like to, but we married late. I'm already fifteen and Joanie is sixtee—!" A jab in my ribs stops me from revealing her age. Dr. Collins chuckles. Joanne rises and helps Dr. Collins settle his old bones into a chair.

"Yes," he says with a weary sigh, "raising children gets more difficult as you get older."

"You've got that right," I say as my mood lightens, "When Timmy was born last year, it was so easy to handle him. Now my back screams at me every time I pick him up."

"How are you feeling?" my wife, ever the caregiver, asks him. "I heard you were having some heart trouble?"

"Nothing serious, my dear. We're long lived in my family. Both my parents made it well into their thirties."

"My goodness." She grins. "We should all be so blessed."

"However, I have to admit I can feel myself running out of steam lately. I am making some changes in my life. That's what I wanted to talk to you about." Dr. Collins smiles at me, "I've decided to retire. I'm recommending you as my replacement."

My jaw drops. Me? Head of Biogerontology?

"I take it that's a 'yes'?" His wrinkled face crinkles in amusement and his laugh lines deepen. I've always marveled at his ability to stay cheerful.

"But, but, you can't retire. None of us have your experience, your—"

"Where do you think I was when I took over from Old Man Henderson? I've spent half my life in research. Now that I've finally become a grandfather, it's time for me to enjoy my few remaining months with my family."

Dr. Collins holds his cane between thumb and forefinger, gently swinging it like a pendulum. The famous smile, that had never wavered through every setback, every failed experiment, drops away like the mask it was. He lets me see his sad, tired old eyes as they settle on mine. We share a silent moment in the midst of the inane conversation around us.

"Spira mirabilis," he murmurs under his breath.

Spira mirabilis, "marvelous spiral." A poetic name for the logarithmic curve first described by Descartes. That elegant mathematical progression is the only piece of data generations of researchers have been able to determine about our decline: how long we had left. Not what. Not why. Just when.

Marvelous spiral, indeed. All I could think of looking at that graceful spiral was the human race, circling the drain. And now I am in charge of stopping it. I don't have a clue how. No one does.

We pause as Bob and Edith Sloan come to say their

goodbyes. As they depart some of our guests join them. Mrs. Sloan seems to have found some followers.

"Can you believe that?" Joanie shakes her head in amazement.

Dr. Collins' gaze is thoughtful. "People look for solace where they can find it."

Joanie is solidly in the science camp. Me, I try to keep an open mind. I wonder about Edith Sloan's biblical quotes. Was it possible the human lifespan had been shortened by another progeroid syndrome in the distant past? I make a mental note to double check with Paleo-osteology.

Dr. Collins braces against his cane and rises, stiff joints creaking. "Well, it's getting late. I should head home as well." He turns to me. "I'll go over the details of your new position with you tomorrow. Congratulations."

The party winds down. It's harder to stay up late now that weekends have been cut to only a day long. How soon before we do away with them altogether?

We show the last of our guests out and briefly celebrate my promotion with another glass of wine. We make a cursory attempt to tidy up before fatigue overwhelms us.

As I climb into bed, we share a long kiss goodnight. I close my eyes and as Joanie drifts off to sleep I'm left in the loneliness of my mind. The fear comes, threatening to swallow me once again. I remind myself of my words to my son and try to find peace.

*For **Orin Kornblit**'s bio, see* The Lurker, p. 20.

The Playground

T.S. Kay

"Wake up! Wake up! We have work to do!" Applejax shook Dickie.

"I don't wanna wake up. Leave me alone!" Dickie turned away from the small boy standing over him.

"Get up now! You don't want them to take someone else, do you?" said Riva, stamping her foot impatiently and tossing her curly, long, blond hair over her shoulder.

"No, that would be bad!" Dickie rolled to his feet. He brushed the leaves from his pants and shirt, looking at the surrounding trees and their lengthening shadows. The sun had just set.

Riva frowned with impatience.

"We have to get to the playground soon," Applejax said, his voice soft and high-pitched. Twice before Applejax had been late waking up. The first time Riva had made friends with him. The second time Dickie had joined them. None of them wanted any more friends. Not that way.

"Okay, let's go." Dickie climbed out of his ditch surprising them. Dickie didn't like to move so quickly when he first woke up.

Applejax took Riva's hand and the two of them skipped after him.

Dickie waited for them by the side of the highway and took Riva's other hand. She smiled.

They crossed the four-lanes, walking quickly despite their size. They didn't worry about cars anymore, at least on this side of the gate.

On the other side of the highway, they passed the storm drain where Riva slept. She pretended passing it didn't bother her but the boys knew the truth. They also couldn't help it. They had to pass it to get to the playground. Applejax had been here first, always woke up first, then woke up Riva at her grate and then they both came for Dickie.

They climbed up the hillside from the roadway and through the hole in the fence. The houses on the other side were silent and dark, as usual. They approached Applejax's garage. His steps slowed to a stop here; they always did.

"Do you like my dress?" Riva asked and twirled around to distract him. It was the same dress she always wore. Pink and frilly, it was the perfect princess dress for a little girl.

Applejax pulled his eyes away from the garage door to give Riva his pretend smile. "Your dress is really pretty, Riva!"

"Thank you!" Riva smiled back, jumped up and down happily, and grabbed Applejax's hand, pulling him away from the garage, toward the playground. Dickie smiled knowingly and grabbed Riva's other hand. If they reminded Applejax they needed to hurry, it made him mad and he would go slower.

"How many visitors today?" Dickie knew but Riva liked to answer questions, even easy ones.

"Two!" Riva sang out.

"They have to pick us!" Applejax said worriedly, focused again with the garage now behind them.

"They will!" Riva said and started to skip, dragging the two of them until they were giggling and skipping along the sidewalk together.

"You're it!" Riva pushed Applejax's shoulder and ran after Dickie. Laughing, he followed her, yelling wordlessly.

They slowed and walked around the corner to the elementary school. Their laughter and chatter echoed across the fields and parking lots. Other than the three of them, there was no other noise. The roads, houses, and front yards surrounding the school were empty and silent. They wouldn't see anyone else until they reached the playground.

"We better hurry before they choose some other kids," Riva reminded them.

"They better not!" Dickie answered, the mood swiftly changing from giddy laughter to angry silence.

Despite their intentions, their pace grew slower and strides shorter as they approached the school. Each looked into the empty, dark windows of the rooms where they had attended kindergarten, at different times with different teachers. Until they went through the playground gate the windows would remain empty, staring at them. And even afterwards, when they were lit and covered with paper cut-outs and drawings, the teachers and students would be strangers.

They sighed silently and turned toward the playground fence. Whether the students were strangers or not didn't matter.

The last hundred yards were always the worst. Tears rolled down Applejax cheeks. Soon he was sobbing and loudly hiccupping. Within a few minutes, all three were wailing. They hated this part.

"Come on, you guys! We have to!" Just as Applejax was always the first to cry, Dickie was always the first to recover.

"Remember, the next part is the best, where they pick us and not the others." Riva reminded herself and them.

"Yeah! Like going to the doctor for a shot and eating ice cream afterwards!" Dickie added.

"Strawberry ice cream!"

"Chocolate!"

"Tutti fruity!"

The three giggled again as they chanted "tutti fruity," and approached the break in the chain-link fence. Where they stepped off the sidewalk, the ground between the two poles was bare, packed dirt.

On the right side of the playground was the back half of the elementary school where the cafeteria and gym were. On the left side was "The Woods", a shadowed place the children dared one another to go after dark. Riva and the others regarded the woods without fear. It couldn't scare them anymore.

The empty playground held their undivided attention. They wished they could spend all of their time there but it was only possible when there were visitors. The slides, swing set, everything were all the perfect size for them. The paint on them was always bright and fresh. The only sound came from the swings as they shifted and creaked in the faint breeze.

They stood before the gate to playground, hand-in-hand, looking at one another and then away, and waiting for one of them to gather the courage to go first.

"I'm hungry!" Applejax declared with a toothy smile.

"Whoopee!" Dickie yelled and did a little dance around the

other two. Soon they joined in. When Applejax was in this kind of mood, it made their work even more fun. Once they got through the gate.

"Let's go" Riva said, grabbing both their hands. Dickie nodded and grabbed Applejax's other hand. They moved closer to the gate.

"One!" Dickie called out, pretending he wasn't afraid.

"Two!" Riva yelled angrily, thinking about the other boys and girls.

"Three!" Applejax whispered with his eyes shut tight as they stepped through the opening.

The tall, white man in the baseball cap approached Dickie. "Have you seen my puppy? He ran away a few minutes ago."

He shook his head.

"Are you sure?" The man took a short step toward him. Dickie didn't know him and wanted to move away but the man held out his cell phone.

"Here's a picture of him. Will you help me look for him?" Dickie inched two steps forward to see a cute, yellow-golden puppy in the frame of the phone.

"Isn't he cute? He loves little boys. I bet when he sees you, he'll come running up and give you a lick on your nose." The man reached out and poked Dickie lightly on his nose. Dickie giggled and the man smiled.

Suddenly the man looked over his shoulder.

"Did you hear that? That's his bark!"

The man took a step away, then stopped, looking back at

Dickie.

"Will you help me? I know he won't run away if he sees you."

Dickie took a step towards the man, then hesitated. Mommy told him to stay away from strangers. He looked around the playground but didn't see her.

"Please? I know he's right on the edge of the trees. I'm sure he's really hungry and thirsty. Won't you help me?" The man held his hand out to Dickie.

Dickie nodded and took the man's hand.

✍

"Momma, I don't want to go with him. I want to stay with you!" Riva stamped her foot, trying to get her mother's attention. It was dark out with no one else in the playground but Riva, her mother, and her two men-friends.

"Mr. Bob bought you that pretty dress. Now do what he says, Riva."

Riva frowned. Momma was acting silly again, closing her eyes, dropping her head, and talking funny.

"I don't want to!"

Momma reached out and grabbed her arm so hard it hurt.

"Go or I'll beat you black and blue!"

Riva whimpered when Momma let go. Riva didn't know what to do, Momma never hurt her before.

"Princess, you're so pretty, I could just eat you up!" The chubby man said with a smile and rubbed the spot on her arm. "You come with me so your momma can be nice to my friend." He held out his hand and Riva nodded fearfully, holding out her own.

∽

"Jacky! Jacky, where are you? Come out, come out, where ever you are! It's play time!"

Applejax was hiding in his secret place in the garage. He hated his cousin Robby and the games he made Applejax play when he babysat. He was so stupid, he kept calling Applejax by the wrong name.

"Jacky, you know I'm going to find you. Come out now and you'll like the game better," Robby called out, his playful voice becoming angry.

Applejax heard the creak of the ladder as Robby climbed up. He shrunk further back into the space between the attic flooring and sloped roof. His heart was pounding so hard, he was sure Robby could hear it. He whimpered when he saw Robby standing over him.

∽

The three friends looked at one another and smiled. The worst part was over. They wiped the tears from their eyes and looked around. It was time for the best part now.

The playground was bright and sunny on this side of the fence. It was full of children playing on monkey bars, the merry-go-round, and slides.

"It's still nice out! We have time," Riva said, looking to see if the other two agreed.

"Yay! Let's play", Dickie and Applejax shouted together.

"I call the swings!" Riva yelled as she ran.

"Slide!" Dickie giggled as he skipped to its steps.

"I want the rocking-horse!" Applejax cried and ran over to it.

There were children already playing on each but as they got close, the other children drifted away, choosing somewhere else to go. No matter how many times they tried, the other children never saw them or stayed to play.

It wasn't long before the wind picked up and clouds blocked the sun. Dickie giggled and Riva laughed and swung higher and higher. Applejax smiled widely and rocked harder on the horse. The visitors were here.

Dickie pointed from atop the slide.

"One!"

The others looked at the gate. There was a large, dark shadow on the other side.

"Two! Two!" Applejax called out excitedly and pointed to the edge of the trees. There was another dark shadow waiting.

"Come out, come out where ever you are!" Applejax chanted.

The wind blew harder, throwing leaves up into their faces. They closed their eyes laughing and giggling as though being tickled. Riva opened her eyes and kicked her legs delightedly when she saw the shadow, now darker and taking shape, cross the gate and approach the playground. Dickie's crazy giggle made her laugh.

"I'm hungry!" Applejax called out in a silly, high-pitched voice and pointed to the other shadow crossing the small field. Riva and Dickie laughed and repeated his words in their own funny voices.

As each shadow drew closer, the darkness deepened from the ground up, and solidified. Then the shadows lightened, changed colors, and became men. The one from the trees was small, thin, and bald. He was wearing black pants, a blue shirt, and a tie. He sat down on a bench off to the side of the swings. He looked around the playground, looking at each of the other children but repeatedly at a young girl with long straight hair swinging on the next set over from Riva.

"You'll like curly hair better!" Riva said, jumping off her swing and running up to the other little girl. She touched the swing's chain and watched enviously as the girl got off the swing and told her friends she was going home. Riva heard her friends decide to go home as well.

The shadow from the gate became an old man with white hair and a beard. Dickie watched him as he looked around the playground and sat on a bench by the merry-go-round. The old man's eyes flitted around, looking everywhere for other grown-ups as he focused his attention on a little boy sitting alone and sad on the merry-go-round.

Dickie laughed loudly when he understood the old man was pretending to ignore the little boy. Dickie skipped over to the merry-go-round and sat down next to the boy. He laughed again when the boy got up and walked slowly away.

"I hope you have a puppy at home to make you happy!" Dickie called after him.

Applejax, Riva, and Dickie made sure not to look either of the men in the eyes. It was too soon for that, it might scare the men away before they could hold hands with them. They stayed where they were, playing, waiting for all the children to leave and for the men to come talk to them. Dickie returned to the slide, knowing by then the old man would follow.

"Hello," the old man said to Dickie, coming to stand at the bottom of the ladder. "You've been going up and down that slide for a long time. You must like it a lot."

Dickie nodded his head, sat down on the slide, and pushed off. When he reached the bottom, he walked back. The old man stood between him and the ladder.

"You must be getting tired. I'm surprised your Mommy hasn't told you it's time to go home."

Dickie shrugged and walked around the man, smiling as he watched him look around the playground for Dickie's family or friends. He heard Applejax giggling in the distance and had to bite his lip so he didn't join in as he climbed the ladder.

"Hi there, cutie!" The bald man said to Riva, sitting on the swing next to her, twirling from side to side.

"Hello," Riva replied, swinging higher and giggling.

"What's your name?" His eyes followed her, back and forth. Riva kicked her legs but didn't reply. He licked his lips and swallowed heavily.

"You really like that swing, don't you!"

Diva nodded her head and laughed.

"You should see the swing that I have. It's way higher than this one so it feels like you're swinging all the way up to the sky. Would you like to swing that high?"

She laughed and nodded again.

"I live right around the corner. You can try it now, if you want to, really quick before it gets dark and you have to go home." He smiled at her and pointed at one of the homes across the street from the playground.

Still swinging, Riva looked at Applejax. He was smiling and rocking. He laughed and nodded his head without returning her gaze.

"My Mommy's friend bought me this dress. Do you like it?"

Both Dickie and Applejax let out high-pitched giggles.

The bald man's head snapped up and his eyes searched the playground for the laughter. Unable to find it, he took a step away from Riva.

Afraid he might leave without her, she jumped from swing and landed on the ground beside him.

"I'm hungry." Riva let the bald man see her big blue eyes. She stuck out her lip and let tears build up. She ignored Dickie's snicker.

"I have lots of food at my house. Cookies, ice cream, and chocolate. You like chocolate, don't you?"

Riva jumped up and down and clapped her hands in excitement.

The bald man laughed and didn't notice the odd sound her hands made. He turned away from her and took several steps.

"Are you coming? If you don't hurry, you won't be able to have chocolate or play on the swing."

She laughed then ran after him towards the gate.

❧

"It's getting dark. You should be getting home soon, shouldn't you?" The old man looked around the playground. "Where is your mommy or daddy? You're not here alone, are you?"

Dickie looked around the playground, shook his head, and

shrugged his thin shoulders.

"Do you live close by? I will walk you home. I'm sure you're afraid to be alone in the dark."

Dickie shrugged as he climbed the slide again. Off to the side, he could hear Applejax giggling. Unable to help himself, Dickie let out a burst of laughter as he took a seat at the top of the slide.

"Whatcha laughing at, kiddo?" The old man's smile froze when he heard the sound of another child's laughter.

"I'm just happy," Dickie answered, looking the old man in the eyes for the first time.

"Why are you so happy?"

Dickie didn't answer at first, just pushed himself down the slide, holding onto the sides as he went. The old man winced at the screeching sound Dickie's nails made against the slide.

"I'm happy because it's almost time to eat and I'm hungry!" Dickie said, jumping forward and smiling widely. This time he didn't join in the laughter he heard.

"I've got some candy and soda in my car. Would you like some?"

Dickie nodded enthusiastically.

"Right after that, I'll take you to your house, okay?"

Dickie laughed and nodded his head.

"Well then, follow me," the old man said, his bright white hair the only thing visible as he walked toward the tree line.

"Okay!" Dickie called out, giggling again as Applejax ran past him and the old man.

⇜

With each step Riva and the bald man took toward the gate the sky grew darker. The wind picked up, blowing dust and debris. The bald man stopped, concern showing on his face. It had grown too dark to see the other side but Riva knew the bald man thought they were now alone.

Up close to the gate, the air grew much colder. The bald man paused again, looking puzzled. Riva could see his breath. She giggled to herself, knowing he couldn't get away now.

"I'm hungry," Riva told him. "After I go on your swing, can I have something to eat?"

The bald man smiled again.

"You can have whatever you like when you come to my house." He turned back to the gate.

"Wait!"

He turned back to her with a slight frown.

"I'm cold. Will you hold my hand?" Riva looked up at him, took one step closer to the gate, and held up her hand.

"You bet, princess." He reached out, took the next step forward, and enfolded Riva's hand and wrist.

Dickie watched as Applejax ran ahead. The old man didn't see him yet. The playground had grown dark and empty. The wind was blowing and it looked like it was going to rain. That was a good sign. The man was theirs.

The old man took big steps but made sure Dickie remained close behind. He was looking at Dickie when Applejax crossed the tree line. A flash of lightening struck, casting black and white shadows.

The old man stopped, noticing the darkness and wind for the first time. He looked down when Dickie caught up with him.

"Looks like there's a storm coming. Won't your mommy or daddy be looking for you?"

Dickie shook his head. The old man frowned and took a step back toward the playground.

When the old man didn't move, Dickie started to hop up and down.

"I have to pee!"

"Then go home." The old man had turned back to him.

"It's too far! I'm afraid to go alone in the woods," Dickie whined and danced again.

"We can stop and you can go once we get to the trees." The old man stared at him, licked his lips, and walked quickly away. Dickie almost had to run to keep up.

As they got closer to the trees, the air grew colder. Mist rose from the ground and formed into a thin, low fog, unmoved by the blowing wind. The tree branches rattled loudly. Dickie could see Applejax sitting on a branch above where he and the old man would pass.

"I'm scared," Dickie stopped just short of the leaves and tree roots barely visible through the thickening fog.

"Don't stop now. There's nothing to be afraid of in the woods." The old man was only steps short of the trees.

"I don't care! I'm scared! I'm going home if you don't hold my hand," Dickie stomped his feet, pretending he was Riva.

"I'm sorry, I didn't know you were that scared." The old man smiled widely.

Dickie smiled back and walked forward, holding up his

hand.

✍

Riva and the bald man stepped onto the sidewalk on the other side of the gate. He stumbled slightly as he took in the dull grey twilight. Only Riva's grip on his hand stopped him from falling.

"That's quite a grip you've got, princess," the bald man told her. He looked down at her hand and his grip went slack. She held him tightly with grey, shriveled fingers ending in blackened broken nails.

Riva was no longer the blond, curly-haired girl with blue eyes and sweet smile. She was wearing the same princess dress but that was all they had in common. Her skull was covered with paper-thin, leathery flesh with only wisps of dirty, scraggly hair. Her rosy cheeks were now sunken, the eyes shriveled, and lips retracted to show the still-white teeth.

Riva pulled hard on his hand and the bald man let out a scream of pain and fear as his fingers broke and his arm pulled from its socket.

"I'm hungry!" Riva screeched, her voice high-pitched and demanding.

Still in shock and unable to understand what was happening, the bald man didn't move fast enough to stop her from wrapping her grey arms around his leg and sinking her teeth into his thigh. He screamed again as she bit through his slacks and into his flesh. She yanked out a chunk with a shake of her head.

She pulled her head back further ripping his pants,

exposing more leg. He fell down hard on the ground trying to crush her but felt her teeth sink in. He whined in terror as her claw-like hand pushed further up his leg.

∽

The old man knew something was wrong the moment he and Dickie stepped onto the leaves around the trees. He shoved Dickie away and started to run. He took three steps when Applejax let out a yell and dropped onto his shoulders and head.

"I'm hungry!" Dickie ran to the old man with whoop. He jumped and knocked them all to the ground.

The old man squirmed around and got his hands on Applejax's throat and shoulder to push him away. He yelled when he saw the mummified child with razor sharp teeth above him.

Applejax shoved a hand into his mouth and giggled when the old man tried to bite through his wrist.

Applejax pushed his thumb into the old man's left eye. It made a squishy sound when it came out of the socket.

"Yum!" Applejax called out and popped it into his mouth.

Struggling under Applejax's attack, the old man arched his body off the dirt and leaves. Behind him, Applejax could hear Dickie slurping and giggling.

Applejax licked his thumb, turned and watched as Dickie reached into the old man's chest through a hole in his stomach. When Applejax stuck his thumb in the old man's other eye, the old man twitched violently then stopped moving.

Dickie and Applejax moved back to make sure the man wasn't faking it but his chest stopped moving.

"Why'd you kill him so fast?" Applejax accused him. "He could have taken another boy or girl! He deserved to hurt more!"

"I know! I didn't mean to!" Dickie protested and kicked the dead man's face.

Applejax shook his head, Dickie always got carried away and ended it too fast. They watched as the body shriveled, looking like them, only bigger. Then the flesh and clothing broke off the skeleton and the bones turned to powder. The now gentle winds blew it all away until there was nothing left. Just them, the leaves, and the trees.

"Come on, let's go find Riva!"

They took off, grinning, for the playground gate.

She was standing over the chewed up body of the bald man.

"Another bad man stopped," she smiled at them.

They watched quietly with her as it turned to dust.

"I'm sleepy," Applejax said.

"Me too," Riva agreed. They walked back past the playground, elementary, middle, and high schools. At first they skipped and played tag but as they got closer to Applejax's garage, they got quieter and their steps slower.

"G'night Applejax!" Dickie called out to him as he walked up his driveway. Applejax turned back and waved before stepping into and through the garage door.

Riva and Dickie walked hand-in-hand across the street then down the hill to Riva's drain. Dickie watched patiently as Riva closed the grate behind her.

He climbed up the embankment and into the wooded area. He walked over to his ditch, sat down into the leaves, then lay down.

"I'm hungry!" He whispered, smiled, and fell asleep.

T.S. Kay is the author of several short stories and novels in the Gifted World, including the soon-to-published, Familiar Scents, *from DAOwen Publications. He grew up an avid reader, loving books, bookstores, and libraries. He worked in a library for seven years where he met the love of his life of more than three decades. Also an education junkie, he has a doctorate in psychology, a master's degree in business administration, and a certificate in military education. He has had more than twenty different jobs but has spent the majority of his time as a consultant to business, a business owner, and a researcher. Dogs have been a part of his life and he and his wife currently share their home with three. Their personal space is encroached upon by more than a thousand frog figurines they've collected from around the world. To learn more about him and his publications, like his Facebook page, www.facebook.com/tskaywriter.*

North

KJ Kabza

They swore it would be different across the wasteland. Here, the last survivors were dying of thirst, but the other side—that would be an oasis, with springs. Streams, even.

Classical texts were consulted and we refurbished ancient engines. Our ambitious odyssey: 12,000 miles and nine months long, across rifts and ridges, across death made of sand and rock. But oh, the stars out there. How they blazed with so little atmosphere.

And still they blazed, 12,000 miles later. We found nothing at the North Pole. No ice. Not even a drop of water. Only an abandoned radio transmitter array, its lonely dishes blasting our ancestors' plea heavenward:

Help. Our planet is dying.

Is anyone listening?

*For **KJ Kabza**'s bio, see* Sputnik 2, Interior, *p. 2.*

Burning Time

Pam Phillips

The Danh, a Filla, and a mental stowaway are riding down our space elevator. The Danh is returning from her journey to the orbitals where she consulted with the Fillas about the solar crisis. One Filla is coming with her as an emissary, and it chafes under what it's agreed to wear: layers of clothing tailored for maximum dignity and minimum comfort, skin tinted to resist the sun, deep eyes, passionate lips, sculpted muscles, a full ensemble of humanity draped on its aluminum frame. Nor does it — no, he, the flesh insists — like losing access to his data feeds and allowing the flesh to decide what's important. The flesh is supposed to let him talk to the Danh, but just now his body seems be concentrating on teaching him to comprehend suffering. He tugs at his collar. "Is my input out of calibration, or is it hot in here?"

"Sun swallowing the Earth and he wants to know if it's hot." The Danh fans herself languidly. And by languid, we mean controlling the speed of the fan by draping her pinkie finger over a joystick. By fan, we mean a contraption that resembles steam-powered scaffolding waving the wings of a megostrich. By her self, we mean possibly the last monarch in Earth, flaunting a costume that dates back, jewelry and all, to the days of unenhanced humans. Sheathed in pleats of white linen and belted with a green band shaped like two snakes twining together under her breasts, she lounges on a purple couch of silk quilted in gold thread and studded with pearls under a lotus-columned canopy. Or at least that's what it looks like, and looks are all that matter when you're trying to make an impression. Five billion years we've served you humans and your successors, and la mode de Cléopâtre still hasn't gone out of style.

By us, we mean the tech infusion that you generally call the nanogods. We maintain the elevator with arrays of bioelectronics constantly repairing any disarrays caused by solar radiation. Our hundreds of legs spider up and down the cable, spraying steelsilk on any rips we find. As the ceramic layer shielding the passenger compartment burns, we carry new layers up from Earth's rocky surface like thousands of ant armies. It's all a strain, but no more painful than your own skin dying from the outside and growing from the inside.

On the inner walls of the passenger compartment, we display images of the realities within our reach. To make it easier for the Danh to guide us, we color-code the frames. More and more of the codes are red, as we surf the waves of possibility away from realities where asteroids hit the Earth, or geologic convulsions crumple the biosphere, or technospawn wipe out the DNAspawn. We need more time to reach to the green-coded realities where life in Earth is still possible. Life means you down there watching us from the underground citydomes, by the way; it hardly seems worth saving the remaining biofilm on the surface of thermophilic poison eaters.

"The Sun is not even close to contacting our orbitals, let alone the Earth," the Filla says. "The actual envelopment won't happen for thousands of years."

The Danh presses gold-lacquered fingernails against the throb behind her eyes. "Oh, you know what I mean."

We do know what she means. We know how she feels, just as we know what the Filla is thinking. Through the synaptic quantum interfaces in your minds, we know how all of you think and feel. We see you watching the focus of our attention, whether in anxious, chattering groups gathering in parks under skywindows, or alone in the depths of the world. We know how many of you are holding our observations in your consciousness, how many are diverting yourselves otherwise, and how many have just shut everything off and are waiting for the end. We're everywhere that you can go, most places you can't, and many places you don't want to go. We're in places we don't want to go. Like the Danh's hangover.

She shifts her red and white crown, trying to ease its weight. We would describe it in more detail, starting with the obvious, like the eagle wings and the cobra, and their heritage and meaning, and how much research we did for her, but all that matters is she gets to wear the tallest hat in the world because she's the Head of the Party. Night after night, or day after day, depending on when you join, she leads you from sacred cave to pleasure dome, in a naked blur of dancing and intoxication, until your perceptions of time slow to a crawl in the search for the endless moment. When you find that moment we stretch it out to give you more time. But as the Sun grows, all her dancing and all your ecstasies haven't found enough.

The Filla flexes his hands and studies them critically. His predecessors built themselves into mechanical housings to get away from the imprecision of things like hands. In the back of his mind, a thought stirs that doesn't quite belong to the Filla: the stowaway we detected when he entered the passenger compartment. The thought gels into a porcine image scratching the buds of its wings against the bars of doubt. But the Filla ignores the thought, attributing it to a hallucination caused by wearing flesh. "If you hadn't asked me to wear this outfit, I wouldn't need to ask what you mean."

"You know perfectly well that we can't wait for the Sun to reach us before we do something," the Danh says. "You're the ones flinging comets around trying to nudge us all out of the way."

For their part, the Fillas are bringing in comets and trying to shift the orbital mechanics of the Earth outward. But their effects are too small and too slow. It's not enough. "The Sun is performing outside our specifications."

"Says the man who thinks we have thousands of years."

He wants to dispute nearly every word in that sentence, so he starts at the beginning. "I am not a human man."

"And we are not monkeys." The Danh snaps upright so that even seated she is looking down on him. As she remembers the game the Fillas suggested, our mood sinks. Is she really going to bring that up? Yes, she is, her thoughts tell us. So we dismantle one of the feathers in the fan, and pieces of us fly to her. She lifts her hands to receive a cascade of tiny green monkeys riding on shiny cans. The monkeys blink and peep to attract her attention. As they chitter and wave their tiny hands, some bounce, some cling, all whirl, falling into many layered rings around her head. The Danh rolls her eyes at the cartoon they represent of the bits of life tended by the Fillas around the Earth. "What sort of a game did you think this was?"

"A collaborative entertainment to solve our mutual problem," the Filla says. The goal being to move the whole system in an orderly manner.

"It's a thinly disguised model!" She's still not sure which is more offensive: the implication that people won't deal with an issue until it's turned into a game, or being asked to pretend she is the size of a planet. She plays a few rounds with flicks of her fingers, glances of her eyes, and whispered cheat codes. The rings widen, make more room, but the moment she turns her head, the system breaks down into chaos, monkeys knocking against each other into red blots of failure.

The Filla feels the bleakness of yet another unpleasant emotion sweep over his thoughts. Whether game or model, it was the latest in a long line of attempts to find an acceptable solution for what would happen to the orbital habitats of the Fillas when they moved the Earth. And there seems to be no way to win. "You made your moves with too much haste. Give it more time."

"I'm making all the time I can," the Danh says.

"You are only stretching time," he says. And it's not doing the Fillas any good. Their devotion to objective reality has been keeping them out of our reach. They have tried to work with us and with the Danh, but they still don't believe that we can save you or them or anyone. The image of doubt in his mind swells to bursting and out pops a pinky-white piglet with stubby wings. We are so excited to see his stowaway emerge, we gather the casualties from the monkey game and give it substance. But the Filla tries to stop us from hacking his thoughts, and claps his hands over his ears. "Unauthorized access!"

Round as a rubber ball, the pig plummets and the Danh catches it on the first bounce. "But this is darling! I didn't think you had it in you."

The Filla lowers his hands in disbelief. "You approve of that creature?"

"I love it," she says extravagantly.

What she loves, we love too. So we decide make it a real pig. We strip excess matter from the screens on the walls; only one reality concerns us. As the screens melt down, the Filla cries out in alarm and leaps to the panel reserved for manual overrides. He slaps it with wide-open palms. "How do I output with these things?"

We are too busy to answer. We burrow through the piglet's skin, constructing plausible joints and a new pair of shoulders. It shudders and groans as it comes to life, clambering up her chest. When it discovers how to beat its wings, it frantically buffets her in the face. Clucking at it to be quiet, she pulls it down to her hip and pins it under her arm, where it squirms like an uncomfortable truth.

By now, we have stripped the passenger compartment to the minimum: a capsule with clear walls that no longer hide what we are up against. We are still high in the atmosphere. Even shielded by the entire mass of the Earth, we can't escape the heat. The sky burns with overflow from the corona, and prickles of green and purple auroras ripple from horizon to horizon.

The poor little piggy trembles and buries its snout in the crook of the Danh's arm. She strokes it tenderly, looking down at deathly light shimmering over a blasted landscape dotted by circles, the only visible sign from this height of the nearly buried spheres where you survive. Music swells in her heart that would sum up all the wild pageants she has danced to lengthen the time we have left. She wants to sing a terrifying aria backed by an orchestra of thousands.

The Filla looks at the sky, where the orbital habitats outshine the stars, super-reflective in a vain attempt to stay cool. Without data tags to mark out which ones have served him as bases of operation, he feels rootless and alone. He cannot see where the other Fillas are roaming around the outer planets. If he fails and the Sun swallows the Earth and consumes the Fillas nearby, the Fillas who have spread to the outer worlds will live. His death will only be one among millions near the Earth, but he still cares and he hates being afraid.

To our surprise, we feel our audience grow in an unexpected direction. Where the image of doubt was lodged in this singular Filla's mind, a channel opens, and the Fillas send a communication that even though he wears a nonstandard body, he is not alone. They inserted a back door to his mind, so they could directly follow his perceptual feed. How sweet! We didn't think they cared.

That's when the shield around our elevator cracks. A wound opens in the wall around a throat of searing flames. Its edges grimace like lips forming the words, *This does not look good*.

As the crack grows, the news spreads among you faster than physical fire. We feel another surge in audience. Good. The more of you and the Fillas who observe this experience, the more power you give us to find the best possibilities, the more we assure ourselves that we have the resources to deal with this.

But the Danh has her own ideas about what to do with the resources available. She begins to hum the music in her heart, low and rhythmic, as she purposefully unties the fake beard on her chin. She feeds it to the piglet. Her crown is next and the intricately braided wig comes with it, revealing a dense bed of tightly cropped hair. Each motion of the hungry jaws seems to take longer to grind costume into flesh. "Help me with the wings," she says to the Filla.

The Filla doesn't believe for a second that she seriously means modifying the wings on the pig. He does spend about 100 milliseconds considering that possibility. His first rough estimate finds that there isn't enough matter available to fabricate wings for even the smallest piglet to carry itself. Having discarded that idea, he spends the next 300 milliseconds reversing the result to estimate how much material he needs to build the simplest possible aerodynamic surface. In 250 he calculates how much time to construct it, and in 50 he takes a readout of their elevation and computes the time before hitting the surface. Not enough. By then the flesh has caught up to his calculations to say, *Stop thinking and do something!*

"This is impossible!" he says. With a snarl, he rips off the skin on his hands as if it were gloves.

Ducking the blast of heat pouring from the wall, the Danh collects scraps of skin and feeds those as well to the little pig. The Danh breaks apart all her fanciful accoutrements. The fan goes into its jaws, the canopy, pieces of the couch. With every bite of matter that it eats, the piglet swells into a pig.

Meanwhile, the Filla is generating code as fast as he can. He jams the digital probes of his manipulators directly into us.

Agony!

We could bear the pain of our walls tearing; that's an expected malfunction, but this! We writhe, cracking the walls further. He seizes our material and with his bare wires infuses his commands. A parafoil he shapes, a harness, and still he takes from us.

Stop, stop! we plead into his language interface. *Why do you think we're going to fall? The cable is still sound. We can't deploy the escape capsule if you —*

But he's not listening on that channel. Someone put too much flesh on the Filla, and his fear is in control. All the other Fillas are watching now, but their chatter overwhelms any communication in a roar of terror. This particular Filla hears nothing but panic, and he redoubles his efforts. No source of material is beyond his demands, not even the cable. A strand snaps.

Oh, shit.

From you below the ground, to the Fillas above the sky, in one collectively held breath, the endless moment the Danh seeks finally arrives.

With the beliefs of humans and Fillas combined, we form a chronopause higher than we've ever reached before. Above that boundary, time runs as it always does. From our viewpoint, from your viewpoint, from the Fillas' viewpoint, time beyond the chronopause seems to run faster and faster, bringing you the spectacle of the Sun rising and setting, rising and setting, rising and setting, faster and faster, until it paints the glowing band that constitutes the Light of the Future.

Inside the chronopause, time stops. Inside the burning passenger compartment, up and down the cable poised to fall, all around the terrestrial sphere, time stops. Even the orbitals pause relative to the Earth's center in a universal geosynchronous city. Wrapped in the moment of the Eternal Now, the world comes unglued from the objective timestream.

In the reality outside the chronopause, the first of the Fillas' comets arrives. Exchange of momentum nudges the Earth a little further away from the Sun. Since neither time nor heat can cross the chronopause, the comet dissolves around it into ionized water vapor. At thousand year intervals, another comet comes. Then another. And another. Every time, we guide the Earth to the best of all possible realities. It's just another way we've been caring for you all these billions of years. What's a million or two to shepherd the Earth to safety? Especially with such a view.

Thriving, vibrant Mars is a blue-green dot of hope growing fatter as the Earth approaches. The Milky Way provides a background for the rich bracelet the Fillas have woven out of asteroids. On this scale, the Jovian moons aren't so far away and the rings of Saturn beckon.

That should be far enough. Gently, we allow the chronopause to thin out, the differing realities to congeal. As time flows down to Earth, we return our attention to the broken space elevator.

The endless moment gives way to the next one. The Filla finishes building his parafoil. The pig grows to full size and stretches its wings. The Danh lifts her hand, looking out through the translucent wall and gasps.

The sky is full of stars. A pale light from beyond the horizon glows within layers of noctilucent ice clouds. Instead of the ghastly light of a dying Sun, the glassy covers of the domes in the ground glow from below with street lights wearily flickering after a long, hard night. She lifts her hand to the rip in the wall and feels a cool breeze. A drop of water lands on her lips.

"What just happened?" the Filla says. His head finally clears enough of emotion to let in frantic transmissions from the other Fillas. They download the final image they received of the damaged wall and how minimal it was before he tore everything apart. They demand an accounting of how his actions could have possibly led to these results. He reviews what happened in the compartment, the tear, the urgency, the request for wings. Completely incomputable. She could have killed them all! Unable to reconcile these recent events with his conception of logic, he holds up the parafoil in his metallic skeletal hands. "I didn't have to manufacture this flying apparatus."

"Well, it was very kind of you," she says. "I so appreciate not dying."

"But we don't need it," he says.

"Of course, we do."

The compartment shudders as another strand breaks, but the Danh tells us to fix it later. She wants to celebrate. Guided by her imagination, we drape the pig in spangles and stars, put a conical hat on its head, making it ready for a flight of fancy dress. The Danh leans forwards and gives it a thorough "good piggy" scritch around its ears. The pig is its own creature now, not our proxy, but if that's how she wants to express her gratitude, we accept. The Danh wraps her arms over its broad round back right between the wings: no longer a sign of doubt, but the impossible achieved. "All aboard!"

The Filla nets the harness around them. Clinging to each other, they jump. The parafoil swells with air. The pig angles its wings to direct their flight into a grand soar. The song within the Danh comes to life. She sings of the night, dark again for the first time in living memory. She sings of the stars, of meteors, of bits of space elevator slashing like fireworks through the sky. With a mighty tremolo, she hails a gentler sunrise. Clouds are rolling in and a chorus of thunder out-sings her.

As they swoop toward a landing, raindrops catch them. Rain is falling all around them. Soon it will strike the ground.

Pam Phillips has been making up odd little stories since she was an odd little girl pretending her fingers were odd little warriors wielding poisonous stingers. Her works have appeared in Wicked Words Quarterly, Used Gravitons, *and* Aoife's Kiss. *She infrequently posts at pamphillips.net.*

Acknowledgments

As with our first anthology, the authors collaborated together to peer-review and workshop each others' stories. We would like to thank them for their continued dedication to producing a strong, collective product.

All proceeds from the sales of this anthology will be donated to the Science Fiction and Fantasy Writers of America (SFWA) emergency medical fund. This fund offers interest-free loans to SFWA members facing unexpected medical expenses.

Talib would like to thank his wife and children for their deep love of reading, which is something he's always hoped he'd be surrounded with. It is amazing to watch the joy his children get from acquiring and reading new books, and it inspires him to create new stories that they may read and enjoy now or in the future.

LJ would like to thank Talib for his endless patience as he kept her on track and wrangled this anthology into being. She is also grateful for the trust of the authors who make up this volume. It was a privilege to be a part of their stories.

47178536R00119

Made in the USA
San Bernardino, CA
25 March 2017